'No. This

Slamming th... ...nd
and reached ... ...ry
desire. '*This* is what I need most.'

He pulled her into his arms and she gasped in
surprise. His mouth closed over hers. She felt
the warmth of his skin through his shirt. It was
a delicious way to be silenced.

'I want you so much,' he said as his hand slid
slowly higher up her stockinged thigh. 'Let me
take you home. Let me make love to you.'

'We can't,' she murmured. 'We must attend the
wedding reception. But I'll make it up to you
when we get home, I promise.'

'No, you can come home with me now and not
attend this blasted reception.'

Sarah Holland was born in Kent, southern England, and brought up in London. She began writing at eighteen because she loved the warmth and excitement of romance novels. She has travelled the world, living in Hong Kong, the South of France and Holland. She attended drama school, and was a nightclub singer and songwriter. She now lives on the Isle of Man. Her hobbies are acting, singing, painting and psychology. She loves buying clothes, noisy dinner parties and being busy.

RED-HOT LOVER

BY
SARAH HOLLAND

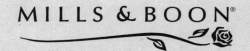

For Mitch Murray

First published in Great Britain 1998
Harlequin Mills & Boon Limited,
Eton House, 18-24 Paradise Road, Richmond, Surrey TW9 1SR

© Sarah Holland 1998

ISBN 0 263 80742 8

Set in Times Roman 11 on 12 pt.
01-9804-46695 C1

Printed and bound in Great Britain
by Mackays of Chatham PLC, Chatham

CHAPTER ONE

CLARA stood in the church with tears in her eyes. Jared stood beside her, tall, powerful and charismatic. He was completely against weddings. He disliked them and did everything he could to avoid them. Whereas Clara loved them. Clara was beatific. Clara was floating along on a dream—lost to everything but the beauty of two lives being joined together.

As the bride reached the groom, the music stopped and everyone sat down. Sunlight shimmered over the twinned heads of the young couple. A blaze of light shafted through the stained glass which soared above a golden altar. Sincerity rang in their voices, and their exchanged vows echoed across the stone arches, pillars and walls of the church. It was a brief shining testament to everything most sacred about being human, needing love and joining together in matrimony.

Tears blurred Clara's vision. She drew in her breath and struggled for self-control, but a muffled sob came from her as she felt hot tears slide over her lashes and down her cheeks.

Jared glanced down his arrogant nose at her, heavy eyelids drooping over steel-blue eyes. She suddenly felt the cool touch of his fingers and looked up breathlessly. Was it possible? Had he been moved by marriage at last? Had something in the ceremony melted his cynical heart?

'Your mascara's run,' he drawled.

Blushing crossly, Clara snatched the handkerchief he offered and dabbed at her eyes. He watched her with a mocking smile. But she refused to take any notice of him because this wasn't just any old wedding. No, this was the wedding she had waited all her life to see.

Her best friend Susie was the bride, and Clara had known Susie since the day they'd both arrived at the orphanage at the age of eight. They had become blood sisters a year later, vowing to be in touch with each other for the rest of their lives until they really did become family. Now, here was Clara, at the age of twenty-nine, still playing Susie's 'sister' on her wedding day.

'With my body, I thee worship...'

'Probably the only vow he really means,' Jared murmured beside her. 'And the only one he'll keep.'

Clara smiled, her green eyes lifting with sensual response to his. For all his cynicism, she knew how important lovemaking was to Jared. He was a marvellous lover and made her feel like a pampered pussycat with just one touch of his hands.

They had been living together for two years, now. She'd fallen in love with him the day she met him, and he'd insisted she move in with him almost immediately. Ever since then they'd been locked into a wonderful, intimate relationship which just kept getting better. The only low points were when they were at weddings. It was odd, really, because Jared was usually so even-tempered. But get him close to a bride and groom and he turned into a very different person. Today he seemed worse than usual.

'I now pronounce you man and wife. You may kiss the bride.'

More tears misted her eyes. She sighed and clasped the handkerchief to her bosom. How passionate they were, this bride and groom. She wondered how many children they would have. And she imagined herself becoming a real live auntie for the first time, with little nieces and nephews. Of course, it wasn't the same as having her own children, but she was confident that that would happen one day, no matter what Jared said to the contrary.

'Silly besotted fool. Susie's lovely, but Gareth will regret marrying her.'

'Honestly, Jared,' she whispered back. 'I do wish you'd stop it.'

'You know perfectly well that most marriages end in div—'

'Shh! They're going to sign the register!' Clara looked resolutely ahead as a singer in a blue dress held up her microphone and began to sing. It was that lovely old classic about a wonderful world. She sang so sweetly, and that, coupled with the bride's glowing amber head as she bent to sign the register, brought tears to every woman's eyes. Clara felt her mouth tremble.

'I wish they'd get a move on,' Jared said impatiently.

'Well, they've got to sign the register!'

'I want to listen to the rugby on the way to the reception.'

Clara sighed. Normally he wasn't obsessed by sport, but today England were playing Wales, and, as a Welshman, Jared naturally intended to cheer for his side. The odd thing was that he had spent the last few days rattling on about it as though he was deeply patriotic. Clara had never noticed any patriotism before this particular rugby match. Far from it. He rarely mentioned Wales. While she found his behaviour over the match rather odd, she dreaded to think what a foul temper he'd be in if they lost. Or, worse, if England thrashed them.

Suddenly the bride and groom were at the altar, the organ played and the bells pealed out.

Clara and Jared got to their feet. He towered beside her like a giant. At six foot six, he was more than a whole foot taller than her. Jet-black hair, a tough face and a scar on his right cheek—he was as passionate as he was masculine. His suit was expensive grey teamed with a dark red silk tie, stylishly knotted. Gold cufflinks flashed against crisp white cuffs. He looked just what he was: a multi-millionaire, and one of the most powerful men in Europe.

As soon as the bride and groom had left the church, Jared took Clara's slender wrist in hard fingers. 'At last. I thought it would never end.'

Clara swayed down the aisle beside Jared. Her blonde beauty had always drawn admiring looks from men, but her fame as a television actress drew just as many. Long sunshine-yellow hair fell in curls to her narrow waist and the wide-brimmed cream hat gave her an air of mystery that enhanced her natural glamour. She wore a cream silk dress which hugged her slender curves. And she was ravishing. Her face was heart-shaped. Luminous green eyes invited love. A full pink mouth invited kisses. And Jared was the recipient of those kisses, every man seemed to think, staring at him with a mixture of awe and envy. He was as powerfully masculine as Clara was sensual and feminine.

Outside in the sunlight, the London churchyard was filling up with well-dressed guests. A trestle table stood close to the arched doors, covered in linen, champagne, glasses and silver ice-buckets.

Jared spotted the champagne immediately. 'Perfect! Just what I need after all that romantic nonsense.'

'I thought it was a beautiful ceremony.'

'You would,' he drawled, and strode purposefully to the trestle table to get himself a glass of champagne.

Clara waited by the steps of the church, studying the handsome man who was her lover and the only man she'd ever truly loved. If weddings upset him this much, there didn't seem any chance he'd ever propose to her. Yet Clara couldn't understand why. Jared had such sensitivity and intelligence. He'd moved naturally into love from the beginning, and Clara had barely to lift a finger to find their relationship flowing freely with love and trust. So why, she wondered, should he hate weddings and marriage with equal passion? He was already living with Clara as though they were man and wife. Clearly it wasn't living with a woman that put him off marriage—so what could it be?

He came back, handed her a glass of champagne.

'Here's to getting out of this delightful little church-yard as soon as possible.'

'Honestly, Jared! Why are you so anti-weddings?'

'Because I'm a normal red-blooded male and you wouldn't have me any other way.'

She laughed softly, eyes tracing his handsome face with love. 'Well, I can't deny that. I'm rather partial to your red blood. In fact, it preys on my mind night and day. But seriously, darling—can't you see how lovely all this is? The bride, the bridesmaids, the—'

'Looks like an extravagant waste of money to me.'

'Coming from a multi-millionaire with two private jets, two private yachts and several homes around the globe—'

'I can afford to waste money.'

'So can the groom's family.'

His face tightened. 'Will you shut up about it?' he bit out as anger flared in his eyes without warning. 'I'm sick to death of this damned wedding! You've talked of nothing else for weeks! Let's just get it over with as fast as possible and get home!'

Stunned, she just stared at him, her lips parted in shock. He had been agitated for the last few days, veering sharply between loving behaviour and sudden bursts of temper. She had put it down to the wedding, because he always played up at weddings. But now she wondered if there was something else on his mind. Something at work, perhaps? Maybe even something to do with money. But how could money be bothering him? He had more of it than Midas.

Moving closer, she put a loving hand on his cheek. 'Darling, you will tell me if something's wrong, won't you?' Her eyes scanned his face. 'I mean—you won't just hide it and try to deal with it alone, will you?'

'All that's wrong is that I need to peel that lovely dress off you,' he drawled, and slid one strong arm around her waist, pulling her slowly towards him. 'I've wanted to make love to you since I woke up this morning. But all you could think of was the wedding, the wedding, the damned wedding!'

'I'll make it up to you as soon as we get home,' she promised huskily in his ear.

'Make sure we get home quickly, then.' His mouth moved over her cheek; his breath fanned her naked throat. 'I want you as soon as possible. Naked but for creamy stockings and that hat. I'll enjoy all that lady-like elegance as I push you over the bed...'

She responded instantly, fire in her blood. Erotic images exploded in her mind and excitement glittered in her half-closed eyes. She forgot all about her fear that something was wrong, because now she knew precisely what it was. He needed her. That was all that was bothering him. Her body curved seductively against his and she shivered at the touch of his hot mouth on her skin. Eyes closing, head tilted back, she must have looked as though she was already naked in his arms.

'Would you like that, darling?' He let one of his long fingers slide down her naked throat, 'Because as soon as I get you home I'm going to do all of that to you and more—'

'Jared, darling!' Susie's voice rang with happiness as she interrupted their private loveplay. 'Stop seducing my sister in front of half of London!'

Jared's whole body tensed. 'Ah!' he drawled, lifting his head with a tight, set face. 'The radiant bride.'

Clara came out of her sensual reverie with a dazed look in her eyes. She heard the faint bite of his tone. A frown touched her brow.

'That sounds as though you're saying: "Ah! The piranha!"' Susie looked as thrown by his remark as Clara felt. She looked from one to the other, then gave a bright laugh, trying to soften the edge that had crept into the sunny afternoon. 'Surely even you don't begrudge my radiance on what is, after all, my wedding day?'

Jared smiled, but his body was tense and Clara told herself it was because of desire. He often got like this. He was sometimes a walking volcano when it came to physical tension. Many times he had come home from work at the end of a long day and made love to Clara for hours, sometimes four or five times a night. He released emotion through making love...

'Of course not.' Jared's impeccable manners returned and his cool voice said, 'You have my very best wishes and congratulations.'

'Thank you.' Susie beamed.

'I just wish we could all get to the reception as fast as possible,' Jared said with a tight smile. 'That's all. I'd like to sit down, have a drink—'

'More champagne, Mr Blackheath, sir?' An usher popped up, brandishing a jeroboam.

Jared watched furiously as he poured.

'There, you see?' Susie said when the usher had gone. 'You've just been sitting down and now you've got champagne flowing wherever you turn! What more could any man ask for?'

'Privacy. You forget—there are photographers around. I always feel uneasy when they can take pictures of Clara and I without my permission.'

Clara frowned. He didn't mind publicity. On the contrary—he actively sought it. It helped his businesses. Publicity always did. The higher the profile, the more business he attracted. That was the way it worked in any sphere of life, and Jared was nothing if not an arch self-publicist. So why was he lying? More to the point—why was he so tense and edgy? Her instincts were buzzing at her from the back of her mind. But no matter what she did or how she looked at things, she could not find a rational explanation for his agitated emotional state.

Susie bit her lip. 'I'm afraid you'll have to pose for the wedding pictures in a minute. Will that be a problem?'

'The photos,' he muttered thickly, and his hand tightened on Clara's waist as he stood stiffly, his arm around her. 'I'd forgotten about them...'

Concern lit her eyes as she studied him. 'Is anything wrong, darling?' she murmured.

'Why should anything be wrong?' he demanded tersely.

'So you will pose with us?' Susie said at once. 'Oh, good, because I must have Clara in the photos, and it'll be bad luck if you don't stand beside her.'

'Will I have to pose with the whole family?' Jared looked at Susie with a brooding expression. 'I don't want to be here all afternoon. I wanted to leave early so I could listen to the rugby on the way to the reception.'

Susie laughed. 'Not another one. Gareth almost cancelled the wedding when he realised it would conflict with England versus Wales!'

'He ought to be put up against a wall and shot,' Jared bit out thickly. 'Calls himself a Welshman? He should have cancelled the wedding on the spot. I would have done.'

Clara stared at him anxiously, and so did Susie. His remark would have sounded like a friendly joke if he had not uttered it in that hard, biting voice.

'Darling—' Clara worriedly soothed him with her most loving smile '—you can't go around cancelling weddings in favour of rugby matches. Besides—this isn't any old wedding. This is my sister's wedding.'

'She's not your sister,' Jared said harshly. 'She's your best friend, and your relationship is as much a farce as this wedding!'

Breathless, she felt the colour drain from her face as the knife went into her heart. How could you? she thought, pain glittering in her eyes. How could you have said that when you know how I feel about her? Even Susie was too shocked to speak. They both just stood there, staring at him. The sun shone down on the spire of the church rising above their heads to a halcyon blue sky.

Jared looked away. 'Forgive me. I didn't mean that.' Then he drained his glass of champagne and strode to the trestle table to get a refill. Clara stared after him.

'Well…' breathed Susie beside her, trying to make

light of it although her voice was shaky. 'Somebody got out of bed on the wrong side this morning. Talk about grumpy-stump-stump!'

Clara turned slowly. Her fingers were so tense on the champagne flute in her hand that she thought the crystal might break at any moment. 'Susie, I don't know what to say. I'm so sorry. Please forgive—'

'Oh, don't worry about it.' Susie put a hand on hers, shaking her red-gold bridal head. 'You've always said he hates weddings and now I've seen it for myself. I just didn't realise he hated them this much.'

'Neither did I.' Clara looked across the lawn to him again.

Jared seemed to sense her watching him and looked round. Their eyes met. He gave her a long, hard stare then a tell-tale stain of red touched his scarred cheek-bone. He turned away, drinking his champagne. Hiding his expression from me, thought Clara at once. He doesn't want me to know what it is he's feeling. And that's the key to all this, isn't it? she thought suddenly. His feelings are building up like a whirl-wind. If only he'd tell me what they are.

'Maybe it's because it's my wedding.' Susie frowned, deep in thought, as she too looked at Jared, trying to understand why a man who had always treated her with affection and respect should suddenly turn into this hostile stranger.

'But Jared adores you, Susie.' Clara turned back to her. 'He really does. I mean—he hates most of my friends but I know he likes you. He would try to get rid of you if he didn't. You know how possessive he is.'

Susie smiled wryly. 'The men who love you always are…'

'But he's never done that with you. If anything, he's encouraged our friendship.'

'Well, he's not encouraging it any more, is he?'

Clara's lovely face went very still. 'You don't think that's why he said all that, do you?'

'I don't know Clara-Bear.'

Their eyes met and held in poignant affection for a moment.

'If he's trying to break us up, I'll never forgive him,' Clara muttered fiercely under her breath. 'I just won't.'

'Calm down,' Susie said at once, taking her hand again. 'It might be a false alarm. For all we know, he'll stop being so bad-tempered once he gets to the reception.'

'What if he doesn't? What if he—?'

'Susie! He wants to do the photos now!' Gareth called suddenly from across the lawn, smiling and waving as he stood on a mound of grass with his family. 'Bring Clara and Jared, will you?'

'Okay, darling!' Susie called, then turned back to Clara, whispering confidentially, 'I'll leave you to get Jared. But try to hurry him up. The quicker these are taken, the quicker we can all get to the reception.' She glided away.

Clara took a quick drink of her champagne, then turned to walk over to Jared.

She stopped after one step. Her heart somersaulted with sick disbelief. Jared was flirting with another woman. Not just flirting but actively showing sexual interest. And the brunette beside him was lapping it up, thrusting out her cleavage, tossing her long hair and licking her over-painted lips.

I can't believe it, she thought, trembling. He's never flirted with another woman. Never even looked at one. Since the minute they'd met, Jared had only had eyes for her. Why was he doing this? Right in front of her? Right here on Susie's wedding day, when he should have been at Clara's side, sharing her joy and happiness—not behaving like a swine, biting people's heads off then going to flirt with another woman.

Tears sprang to her eyes but she blinked them back. She groped around for her faith in him. He loves me, she told herself fiercely. I know he does. It's just that something's wrong and he can't share it with me. Not yet. Whatever it is, I'll sort it out with him later. Meanwhile, that little man-eater is not getting her hands on my man!

Straightening up fast, Clara put her best foot forward and went over to break up the little tête-à-tête.

'Darling!' Smiling brightly, she slid a possessive hand through his arm. 'Sorry to drag you away, but it's time for the family photos.'

'Must I?' he demanded tightly.

'Yes, you must.' Her heart skipped beats with fear. She was appalled that he could even consider turning her down, especially in front of this seductive stranger.

'Family photos?' drawled the brunette, with a withering glance at Clara. 'What a bore, Jared. I'd decline if I were you.'

'I'm afraid he can't decline,' Clara said thickly. 'You see, the bride is my sister. Jared lives with me and has been my boyfriend—' she enunciated the word 'boyfriend' '—for the last two years. So, he really is honour-bound to appear in the wedding photos.' She tugged at Jared's arm. 'Come along, darling. They're waiting for us.'

Relief overwhelmed her because Jared allowed himself to be pulled away, but his face was very tense and his eyes were dark. In silence they walked across the sunlit churchyard. Birds were singing above the laughter of the guests. The summer breeze was warm on Clara's skin, but inside her heart was aching and hurt.

'I don't want to be in these damned photos!' he muttered beside her, trying to guide her away from the grassy mound they were supposed to be going to.

'Jared, what on earth is the matter with you?' she asked hoarsely, keeping her voice low so no one could hear her. 'You knew you had to be in the photos. I told you weeks ago.'

'Did you? I forgot.'

'You can't possibly have forgotten. I've reminded you almost every day. And don't try to tell me you deliberately flirted with that woman to avoid having your photo taken. You have your photo taken all the time.'

'For business purposes.'

'Don't be evasive,' she whispered fiercely. 'You know what you did just now. How could you? How could you humiliate me by flirting with that woman so blatantly?'

'I wasn't flirting with her,' he muttered under his breath, watching his polished black shoes as he walked.

'Yes, you were. I'm not a fool. Nor are any of the people here today.' Hurt flashed in her eyes. 'And you made me feel very jealous. You did that deliberately. I know you did. Why did you do that? What on earth have I done to make you behave this way?'

'I hate weddings,' he bit out thickly. 'I keep telling you that. You should have left me at home and come alone.'

'I needed you with me.'

'You keep saying that, but—' He broke off, stopped walking and studied the waiting group a few feet from them.

The bride, the groom, the photographer and Gareth's family were all smiling across at Clara and Jared. It was an idyllic, happy scene, thought Clara. Everyone looked so good, and the sun was high in a clear blue sky on what must have been one of the hottest days of the year so far.

But Jared's face was pale with tension. And as he stared across at the little family group his breathing altered and his heart began to beat heavily.

He looked around, as though searching for a way to escape.

'Darling…?' Clara whispered with a sudden renewal of concern. 'What on earth is wrong?'

'It's nothing,' he muttered, but as he looked back at the group he drew a harsh breath and suddenly turned to Clara, his arm going around her as he pulled her close and kissed her cheek. As their bodies touched she felt the beat of his heart. Was he frightened? But what on earth could frighten him in this idyllic setting? Yet he was deeply worried about something. Otherwise why would he close his eyes for so long as he kissed her, and why would he let his mouth linger a second too long on the soft curve of her cheek?

Suddenly she was released. But he grasped her hand in his as he led her to the smiling wedding group. One or two of Gareth's family said hello. Jared nodded, gave them a tense smile, but did not speak. The photographer started taking pictures. Clara smiled as Jared's large powerful hand nearly crushed hers—his grip was tightening the longer he had to stand here.

'Could I get one of you alone with Miss Maye, Mr Blackheath?'

'This isn't our wedding day,' Jared said. 'It's Susie and Gareth's, as you very well know.'

'Yes, but it isn't often I get to take a few shots of such a famous couple.'

Clara felt herself blush. She'd always been happy to be famous, and she knew Jared was. It was one of the things they had in common. But to be photographed like this in front of the whole wedding crowd on Susie's wedding day felt uncomfortably like upstaging the bride. Her eyes flickered to Susie's as the rest of the family moved obligingly away, leaving Clara and Jared alone on the grassy knoll, centre stage and in the spotlight once again.

'Go on.' Susie grinned at her approvingly.

Clara bit her lip and looked up at Jared. He didn't

look as happy as she felt. In fact his face was hard, and set in an angry expression. He was also, she noticed, staring across the churchyard at the church, not looking at the bride and the groom or the photographer at all.

'Just one or two,' murmured the photographer, already taking pictures.

'Very well.' Jared's mouth tightened. He stood on Clara's right, still looking at the church, giving the photographer his arrogant profile, refusing to look at the camera or the family. Aware that the photographs would need some kind of composition, Clara looked up into Jared's face with a smile, making the photo double-facing.

He felt her stare, glanced down at her and saw the love in her green eyes. A brief smile touched his mouth. The sun glowed behind them. It must have made a beautiful shot because murmurs of delight went up from the crowd. Clara felt her smile widen—being an orphan had left her with a remarkable desire to be noticed and talked about, as though without public acclaim she somehow did not truly exist. She had often wondered if Jared felt the same. She wondered it again now as she saw the smile deepen on his handsome face, aware of the stir they were causing.

Everyone was watching Clara and Jared. Although Clara was a well-known face from the television, Jared was the big fish. Sexy, dynamic multi-millionaire tycoons were a rarity in any arena. Most people simply stared at him in awe.

'Lovely, thanks.' The photographer wouldn't let up. 'Just one more…'

But before the shutter clicked, Susie called, 'Here!' She threw her bouquet at Clara. 'Your turn next, blushing bride!'

'Right, that's enough!' Jared muttered furiously to Clara. 'No more photographs. We're leaving.' He raised his voice so the others could hear. 'Thank you, but we're very tired and need to go. See you at the reception!'

Without waiting for a reply from anyone, Jared turned on his heel and strode away across the church-yard, still holding Clara's hand tightly so she could not get away from him. Guests scattered like a flurry of flamingoes, all tottering in hats and high heels to let Jared Blackheath pass. And, clinging with one hand to both her hat and her new bouquet, Clara skittered along beside him.

His hatred of weddings had reached an all-time high. But why had this wedding, above all others, provoked it? There had to be some secret ingredient that had gone into today that she didn't know about. But what…?

CHAPTER TWO

OUTSIDE the church, Jared beckoned the limousine. Harrison had been sitting on the bonnet in his grey uniform and peaked cap. He had a half-eaten sandwich in one hand, a cup of coffee in the other and a steel flask resting precariously on the bumper.

'He's having his break, poor man,' murmured Clara as Harrison fumbled around trying to get ready to leave.

'I don't pay him to make me wait.' Jared strode across the leafy Kensington road without waiting. 'He must have seen us coming out of the church. He should have been ready to leave at a moment's notice.'

Harrison was already behind the wheel by the time they reached the car. He knew his boss too well to even consider getting things wrong when Jared had a face like thunder. Normally even-tempered and good-natured, Jared in a bad mood was not a man to tangle with. And if he had been in a bad mood this morning, before they left for the church, he was in a much worse mood now as he wrenched open the rear door.

Clara slid in first, and shifted breathlessly along the dove-grey seats as Jared got in beside her.

He slammed the door and bit out thickly, 'The Ritz!'

'Very good, sir.' Harrison murmured, but did not turn his grey head to look at his master.

As they drove away down the little Kensington mews, Jared was already shouldering out of his grey jacket. It was a sure sign of severe muscular tension. He frequently did it after a gruelling board meeting, and his next step was always to loosen his tie, which he was now doing. Clara watched for the final step—unbuttoning the top three buttons of his shirt and all the buttons of his formal grey waistcoat. Finally, he leaned back against the seats, with his arms spread out on either side, and closed his eyes.

Clara watched him with concern. 'Would you like me to massage your shoulders?'

'Yes.' It was a curt reply, and she made a face at him while his eyes were still closed because of it. 'I saw that,' he muttered, watching through slitted lids.

'Well, you are in a horrid mood, darling!' she said lightly.

'That doesn't give you licence to make faces at me behind my back.'

'Oh, yes, it does!' she teased, but she also knelt up on the seats to better get to his shoulder muscles. As soon as her fingers began to knead the lock-tight muscles, he gave a deep groan. 'Oh, that's lovely...'

'Does it hurt?'

'Sublimely,' he said from deep in his throat. 'I love it. Don't stop.'

As she massaged and pummelled and pushed and kneaded, she thought about today's wedding and tried to hone in on the secret ingredient that had made it so intolerable for him. He should not, after all, feel as though he'd just beaten his arch-enemies in a grim boardroom battle for power. Most people felt light and happy after attending a wedding, especially one as beautiful and simple as Susie's. If nothing else, it renewed one's faith in love.

And Jared did have a great deal of faith in love. Oh, he huffed the way most men do—particularly powerful men—and talked a blue streak about weddings being 'romantic nonsense' or 'a trap'. But underneath the hard-headed macho façade, Jared hid a deep romanticism that he was afraid to let anyone but Clara know about. He had to keep it hidden. There were too many sharks in the world of big business and he could not risk letting his enemies see how vulnerable he could be. How could such a sensitive man grow to hate weddings so much that he reacted like a cornered animal to them?

'It was worse for you today, wasn't it?' she said gently as his muscles began to unknot and relax beneath her loving fingers.

'I hated every second of it.'

'You always have a bad time at weddings. But there seemed to be something different about today that I—'

'There was nothing different about today.'

'Then why are you so tense?'

His eyes flashed open, watching her with a guarded expression. 'I'm not tense!'

Her pale brows rose.

'I said, I'm not tense!' He flushed angrily and shrugged her off. 'In fact, there's nothing wrong with me that a large brandy wouldn't cure!' Leaning forwards, he clicked open the drinks cabinet.

Clara watched with a frown as he poured himself a measure of cognac. A disciplined man, constantly driven to achieve, Jared rarely drank. In fact, she had known periods of up to four or five months go by without Jared touching even wine. Yet he had so far drunk two glasses of champagne, was now starting on brandy, and it was still only mid-afternoon.

'Are you sure you want that brandy?' she asked softly.

'Quite sure, thank you!' He glared over the rim of the glass.

Clara met his angry gaze and said, 'Give me a smile. You look so grim.'

'Why shouldn't I look grim?' He sat back, drank some more brandy. 'You know I hate weddings. You know they irritate me. And you know I get bad-tempered just sitting through them. But you deliberately dragged me along to this one. Even though I told you this morning that I knew it would ruin the day for us.'

'Darling…' She was amazed that he could continue to be so unreasonable. 'This wasn't just any wedding.'

'You knew it would ruin the day if I came along.'

'But the day *was* the wedding. There was nothing else *to* the day. Just this. The church, the wedding, the bride, the groom—'

'Precisely.'

She drew a patient breath. It was pointless arguing with him when he was in one of these moods. And it was true—she *had* known he would have a difficult time. She just hadn't been able to see a way round it for either of them.

'Well,' she said with a placatory smile, 'the ceremony itself is over. You can relax and look forward to the reception.'

'I don't want to go.'

Clara's jaw dropped. For a second she just stared at him in speechless disbelief. Had he really said that? It wasn't feasible. Not today.

Jared's angular cheekbones ran red as he saw the shock in her face. 'Look—I've had enough. All right? I know I'm not going to enjoy the reception.'

'But, Jared, I—'

'No. I've had enough. Can't you see that?' He sighed, ran a hand over the back of his neck as though the mere thought of the reception was sending his muscles back into a state of rigid tension. 'It's not just the marriage bit that I object to. It's the press attention and the way everyone keeps staring at me.'

Clara found her tongue. 'But press attention and admiring stares have been a part of your life since you first hit adulthood! In fact, you've been famous for over half your life! How can you possibly expect me to believe you've suddenly turned camera-shy?'

'Yes, well, I'm not in the mood for cameras today.'

'Why not?'

'What do you mean—"Why not?"' He threw her a furious look. 'I don't have a reason! I just know that that's how I feel. Today, for my own personal reasons, I hate the attention. I hate being stared at like an animal in a zoo. I hate being photographed. And, most of all, I hate being asked stupid questions by strangers.' He drank some more brandy, his face tense. 'I don't want to continue any further. I want, in fact, to abandon ship. I suggest we bypass the Ritz, turn round at Eros and go straight home. I'll tell Harrison to—'

'No!' The word shot from her like a bullet from a gun and she caught his arm as he moved to lean forward and speak to Harrison. 'Jared, I'm not going to let Susie down like this! She's my best friend. She's the closest thing—'

'I know, I know!' he muttered angrily, and after a second gave a deep sigh as he slumped back in his seat. But he glared straight ahead and refused to look at her. 'All right. All right. We'll go to the reception, damn it all to hell!'

She moistened her lips. 'You don't seriously want us to go home. I know you're only saying it because you're upset. You care about Susie, and you'd never do anything to destroy her happiness. It's just this day, somehow. Something unusual must have happened today that I don't know about.' She was thinking aloud, going over the clues without realising what she was saying. 'Something to do with the wedding photograph. The Llewellyns—'

'Shut up!' he bit out thickly, and when she looked up in startled disbelief at him speaking to her like that, she saw the tide of dark red deepening on his cheekbones.

She also saw the look in his eyes.

The black pupils were fully dilated now. The vivid blue surrounding them was shifting, glittering, ever-changing like a kaleidoscope. She had seen that look before. It meant he was trying to hide something. Suddenly her confused mind began to click certain things into place.

'Have you met the Llewellyns before?' she asked softly.

'The groom's family?' he replied, like a politician, skilfully evading the question, and leaned forward, trying to pretend he hadn't evaded it. 'Their Welsh connection just reminded me that I was missing the rugby match, that's all.'

He switched on the radio while Clara watched him with very thoughtful eyes. He had yet to answer yes or no.

'And England have won!' The commentator's voice burst out excitedly over a roaring, cheering crowd. '5-4 to England, knocking Wales out of the running and wiping the floor with—'

'Great.' Jared punched it off again but was clearly glad to have an excuse to continue in this bad-tempered mood. 'Now Wales have lost. That just about makes my day.'

'Never mind, darling. It's only a rugby match. There'll be others. And besides—we can go and see them play in Wales.'

He tensed and his dark lashes flickered. Clara knew in that moment that all this had something to do with Wales, although she couldn't for the life of her figure out why meeting a Welsh family should send him into such a strange and inexplicable mood.

'Wales…?' he said thickly, staring at her as though she'd just grown two heads.

'Wouldn't it be better to see them play on their own

home ground? We could drive down to Wales for the weekend and have a deliciously private holiday together, as well as supporting the team.'

'Sounds like just what I need,' he drawled unsteadily, avoiding her eyes and breathing a little easier.

Clara could hardly allow them both to turn up at the wedding reception of her oldest friend without first attempting to defuse his intense and explosive feelings.

'Yes, we could go to Wales, watch the rugby, see the sights—'

'What sights?'

'And even visit your mother.'

His mouth tightened. 'Oh, yes...'

Clara frowned, studying him. Three times a year his mother, Lily Blackheath, made the train trip to London alone, staying in five-star luxury at the Dorchester.

A tall, slender and striking woman, Lily had kept her hair dyed jet-black and looked much younger than her fifty-seven years. But she never visited Clara and Jared at their Regent's Park home. Jared didn't want her there and Lily seemed to agree with that. They had a strange relationship, mother and son. Tied to each other by ropes of steel, yet so distant with each other it was as if they were bound by some dark secret. And when Clara tried to probe, they united against her. That was when they really did seem like mother and son. When they joined hands to ward off danger and keep their secret. Of course, Clara could not be sure that that was the case. She could only suspect.

'Well,' said Jared after he'd had a moment to think, 'Lily wouldn't really want us there. She's got her own life. She's a busy lady. She wouldn't want us barging in on her uninvited.'

'Have you ever asked her?'

'Besides,' he continued, as though she had not spoken, 'I'm much too busy with work at the moment. I can't take any time off. Don't forget I'm going to Texas on Monday, then San Francisco. I'll be away for at least a fortnight. And after that there's the usual round of board meetings and London business, and then I'm off to Hong Kong, Tokyo...'

Clara suspected he was dodging the issue, but couldn't prove it any more than she could have done when he avoided answering her question about the Llewellyns. It could be true that he was too busy. He was, after all, a very busy man, with an action-packed schedule. But he was the kind of man who moved mountains when he wanted something. If he wanted to go to Wales and visit old haunts, watch the rugby, see his mother—he would go. But, of course, Wales was a no-go area...

Jared flew to every country of the world except the country of his birth. And Clara's career did sometimes permit her to go with him, to leave London for weeks at a time, travelling the world in stretch limousines and private jets with the man she loved. It was just as exciting as working in television, although Clara couldn't help needing the security that only a career could bring. So she always made sure she kept on working. And her agent, Mitch, was very good at keeping Clara in work as often as possible.

Once or twice a job had come up for her while she was away with Jared, and Mitch had called her with the news, no matter where Jared had taken her—whether Mombasa or Dubai or Venezuela. She had flown straight back for the auditions and got them. But, no matter where Jared had taken her, he had never so much as suggested they set foot in Wales together. Not since the day she met him. Jared's company had offices in almost every capital of the world. Even such far-flung places as Cuba, Taiwan and Latvia were on his annual visiting list. But never Wales. Never Rhossana Bay. Not even to visit his mother.

Now she saw the connection between Wales and Susie's wedding for the first time.

Funny the things you miss, she thought, when your own feelings are so deeply involved, as mine are with Susie. I never gave it a second thought that she was marrying a Welshman. I just thought, What a coincidence that she should love a Welshman, too! And that was that.

But, after Jared's complex and unfathomable reaction to the Welsh presence at the wedding, she knew she must find out what his real reasons were, or there was trouble ahead for both of them. If Jared continued to feel this way about the marriage, she could see arguments looming—most notably at the reception.

For that reason, she pushed on with her pursuit of the subject. It was the only sensible thing to do.

'We ought to go to Wales anyway, even if it's not until next year.'

He rapped long fingers on his thigh. 'What's the big deal about Wales all of a sudden?'

'I still haven't seen the place where you were born. Rhossana Bay, wasn't it?'

'Rhossana is a dead-end seaside town with absolutely nothing to recommend it.'

'That's not what my guidebook says.'

He turned slowly to stare at her. 'You've got a guidebook? On Wales?'

'I bought it as part of a set on the UK when I was trying for that job as a presenter. I had to have a wide knowledge of the country because it was a travel programme on—'

'You didn't need a wide knowledge of Rhossana Bay!' He gave her an arrogant look. 'I could have told you all you needed to know. For instance—it would only take you half an hour to walk from one end of town to the other! It's not exactly the big metropolis.'

'Yes, but as I had the book I took a quick look to—'

'Don't give me that! The truth is, you've been checking up on me out of sheer female nosiness.'

'I admit I was curious, but—'

'Nosy,' he accused, glaring at her. 'Like all women, you assume that there's something wrong with me. That I need fixing and that you're the girl to do it. Well, let me tell you, Little Miss Fix-It, there's nothing wrong with me that another stiff brandy wouldn't cure!'

Clara released his hand as he leant forward to angrily open the cabinet again.

'No. This isn't what I need.' Slamming the cabinet shut, he turned round and reached for Clara, eyes burning with a rush of angry desire. '*This* is what I need most.'

He pulled her into his arms and she gasped in surprise. His mouth closed over hers. She felt the warmth of his skin through his shirt. It was a delicious way to be silenced.

As Jared pressed the electric button which operated the dark screen window between chauffeur and passengers, she realised what he was planning. She gave herself up to it, eyes closed and head tilted back, the kiss stirring pulses in her body. He was stirred too. His hands moved passionately over her. Her hat fell softly backwards, tipped onto the seat.

Clara moaned, pulses quickening rapidly. He was so gorgeous when he was in a temper. Try as she did to soothe him, she really did find him irresistible when he grabbed her like this for a quick, fierce kiss. He pulled her closer. He deepened the kiss and his breathing quickened. Clara's heart was pounding madly. Everything grew dark and sensual. Images flashed through her mind of the four-poster bed at home...

'Oh, Jared...' she whispered thickly.

'Just turning your body on and your brain off, baby!' he muttered passionately against her mouth, and his hand moved up to close over her breast, making her moan as he kissed her deeper, his long fingers stroking her erect nipple through her clothes. 'Like that?'

'Yes... I'm on fire...'

'So am I.' His voice was hoarse and his face darkly flushed with excitement. 'In fact, I want to make love to you—right here and now…'

Moaning, she kissed him sensually. 'Oh, yes, please…'

He gave a rough groan and plundered her mouth. The car was slowing down now, inching through traffic while Jared obliterated Clara with the sheer power of his kiss. His hand was on her thigh, stroking the pale flesh above the lace top of her stocking.

'I want you so much,' he ground out as his hand slid slowly higher up her stockinged thigh. 'Let me take you home. Let me make love to you.'

'We can't,' she murmured through passion-bruised lips. 'We must attend the reception. But I'll make it up to you when we get home, I promise.'

'I'd much rather you made it up to me now.'

'So would I.' She lay back, dazed and flushed and over-excited, her hands in his thick dark hair. 'But we can't…'

'Yes, we can. You can come home with me now and not attend this blasted reception.'

The car stopped outside the Ritz. Jared was watching her intently. His face was dark with sexual excitement, yet the black pupils of his eyes were surrounded by a glittering kaleidoscope of blue which told her he was trying to hide something, trying to get his own way and trying to cope with an emotional chaos she could only guess at.

He was determined to avoid the reception.

Clara tried to get her breath back. He'd always known how difficult she found it to resist him. That was why he'd pulled this stunt just before they reached the hotel. He knew it would put the greatest pressure on her to do as he asked.

'Jared, we're sitting on the top table with the bride and groom. We're here as Susie's only family. We have to attend. There simply isn't any choice. Not for me, at any rate.'

His fists clenched. 'Clara…I want to go home.'

She tried to sit up, breathless. 'Look—Harrison's getting out to open the door.'

'He can just damned well get back in.'

'No, he can't.'

'I want to leave.'

'Jared, Susie is my—'

'I am not attending—'

Harrison opened the door.

Dishevelled and loveswept, Clara hesitated. But only for a moment. Jared was on the brink of ordering Harrison to drive them straight home and she couldn't let him do it. Not at this wedding. Susie wouldn't just be disappointed. She'd be heartbroken. And in that moment of hesitation all Clara could think of was the little red-haired girl in the playground of St Winifred's, who had hurled herself fiercely at the boy who'd just broken Clara's doll. Susie had leapt to Clara's defence on the day they met. The very least Clara could do now was return the favour—twenty-one years later.

Fumbling for her hat and bag, she stepped out onto the hot pavement while Jared watched her with brooding temper. She avoided his gaze. He could glare at her all he liked. She wasn't getting back into the car.

'Clara.' Jared's voice was almost drowned out by the sound of traffic. 'Get back in the car.'

She pretended not to have heard him, and stepped back to let the traffic drown his voice to nothing. Staring resolutely at the curly green writing on the Lebanese restaurant across the road, she continued to avoid his eyes. He was trying to will her back into the car.

Eventually, he got out. Women walking past stared at him with admiring recognition. He stood smouldering with bad temper as he shrugged his grey jacket back on.

Clara turned on her high heels before he could start another argument and walked up the gilded steps to the swing doors of the Ritz.

Inside, the hushed pink and marble shimmered and the soft carpeted reception area glowed under crystal chandeliers. Handsome young men in smart frock-coats swished around attending to wealthy guests.

'Very well.' Jared strode in behind her with a face like thunder. 'You get your way. So where is it? This wedding reception? The Marie Antoinette Suite?'

'No, the restaurant.'

'Then let's get it over with.' He took her hand in a firm grip and strode off down the pink carpet past the Palm Court. People stared. It was at moments like this, when they were in the middle of a blazing row, that Clara wished they weren't so famous.

But as they entered the restaurant her tense face relaxed into a radiant smile. A wedding breakfast fit for a princess, she thought, staring at the top table which ran along the French doors. White lace and satin decorated it; sapphire taffeta bows gleamed along the edges. Silver flatware, an assortment of crystal glasses and bouquets of the most exquisite pale pink orchids completed the look of luxurious celebration.

For a little ragamuffin from St Winifred's—with no parents, family or real chance in life—Susan O'Malley had done well. Susie had not realised when she first met Gareth that his grandfather, Owain Llewellyn, was rich. Gareth's family was so used to money that they were almost aristocratic in their habits: unpretentious, homely and down to earth. Imagine Susie's shock when she'd realised she'd been courting for a year with a Llewellyn of Llewellyn and Sons, Builders—a firm currently valued at over fourteen million pounds and entirely in private hands.

'Looks wonderful, doesn't it?'

'Wonderful.' He strode without another word to inspect the table. Clara followed him. He was reading the place settings. As he reached the far end of the table he caught his breath, staring. 'We're sitting here! Did you organise the place settings? Did you put me—?'

'Of course I didn't.'

'Then who did?'

'Well, I imagine it was the groom's mother. She organised the whole thing.'

'Why was she allowed to?'

Clara's eyes rounded in amazement and he flushed angrily.

'I can't sit here!'

'Jared, for heaven's sake stop behaving like this!

It's only a wedding reception. You won't have to stay longer than an hour or two. Who are you sitting next to, anyway? Let me see the—'

'Owain Llewellyn Senior,' he snapped, and turned on his heel, mystifying her as he walked out of the open French doors into the private gardens beyond.

Clara counted to ten. Keep your cool, she told herself, and picked up the place card. Studying it as though convinced she might find some clue on it, she eventually replaced it, baffled. Then she followed Jared out into the gardens.

He stood with his back to her. Sunlight blazed over his dark hair and made it seem to shine blue-black. A balustrade ran along the white steps which led to the lawns. Grecian urns were bathed lazily in the warmth of the summer afternoon.

'Darling—' she walked up behind him '—why don't you want to sit next to Owain Llewellyn Senior? Do you know Mr Llewellyn?'

Silence.

She tried again. 'Is there some kind of business intrigue going on that I don't know about? Something that's happened between you and the Llewellyns that makes social interaction difficult?' Jared bought and sold companies as part of his work. Failing businesses were turned into dynamic successes with a wave of the Blackheath hand. Because of this, he frequently had to build new factories or redesign existing buildings to accommodate the leap in productivity and employment.

'You know I always use Wright-McArd for all my

construction work in the UK. Why would I engage another building firm?'

'Especially a Welsh firm?'

'It's got nothing to do with their Welshness. You don't seriously think I'd do business on a basis of personal background or family history?'

'I didn't mention family history.'

He tensed, aware he had given himself away.

'Do you know anything about their family history, Jared?'

'What is this—the Spanish Inquisition?' He turned away, his voice thick. 'I couldn't be less interested in the Llewellyns or their family history.'

'Then why don't you want to sit next to Owain Llewellyn?' She knew she was pressing on some kind of old wound but she wasn't going to let him keep his secret hidden for ever. Not when it was so obviously painful for him. To say nothing of the trouble it was causing everyone today. Jared had a tendency to cope alone with difficult emotions. Normally she let him carry on while she waited for the moment he decided to turn to her and share them. But today they simply didn't have time for that approach. 'Let's examine exactly who Owain Llewellyn is, shall we?'

'Let's not,' he muttered, but she carried on regardless.

'The head of the firm. Gareth's grandfather. Just an old man in his early sixties with very little about him that could possibly worry—'

'Stop harping on about him. I'm not interested in the man. Why are you?'

She was obviously getting warmer. 'The Llewellyn

offices are in Cardiff, aren't they? I'm sure I remember Susie mentioning something about it. Offices in London, Cardiff—'

'I don't want to discuss the geographical details of Llewellyn's damned offices!'

'And a house in the countryside. A house by the sea, Susie said, somewhere on the south coast, somewhere Gareth always wanted to visit but wasn't allowed to because…' She paused with a thoughtful frown. 'Now why was that? He couldn't visit the house because his family said—'

'Look!' He turned on her without warning. 'I just don't want to be here, all right? Is that so hard to understand? Must you hunt for clues that don't exist? Stop trying to find a logical reason because there isn't one! I hate weddings! I always have; I always will. End of story. Now leave me alone'.

A bird hopped onto the balustrade, trilled sweetly and regarded them both with beady eyes.

Clara was very still. Jared was determined not to be questioned and that meant she was on the right track. But what lay at the end of the trail? Now that she'd started picking at the Llewellyn subject she was beginning to realise that all his behaviour—from the moment Susie had met Gareth right up until today—could be attributed to the presence of a Welsh family called the Llewellyns. Why hadn't she picked up on that before? If she had, there might have been a chance of helping him cope with whatever he was going through in that battened-down hatch of a heart. As it was, she had left it too late. The breakfast was due to start at any minute. And Jared was getting worse, not better. Although she hated giving up, she knew it was the only wise course of action. There was only one thing she could do. Let him leave.

'Okay…' She admitted defeat with forgiving tenderness. 'I understand. If you really want to leave, then…' she shrugged '…leave.'

He did a double-take, staring. He took a step towards her. His eyes were haunted. 'Are you serious?'

'Darling, I don't want to see you suffer like this. You obviously can't bear to be here. I've tried everything I can to make the day enjoyable for you, but even I've run out of ideas. If you want to go—go.'

He reached for her, pulled her tenderly into his arms and buried his hot face in her neck. 'I can't believe you mean it. You're the most wonderful woman in the world.'

She laughed softly and stroked his dark hair. 'I know, I know! But hurry up, darling. People are arriving. In fact the dining room looks crowded from here.'

'Forgive me,' he muttered deeply and raised his head, love in his eyes as he stared down at her. 'I've behaved so badly today. But if you only knew what a strain it's been for me. The last few months, weeks, days…'

'You've been hiding your real feelings from me all along, haven't you? Darling, you mustn't do that. It upsets me and doesn't help you.'

'I promise not to do it any more. Starting from now…' His mouth closed over hers in a slow, gentle kiss. Clara gave herself wholeheartedly to his loving embrace, letting her head fall back so that her hat dropped softly to the ground. They both ignored it. Her mouth opened beneath Jared's and the kiss took fire.

'We'll go straight home and straight to bed!' he muttered roughly, and she tensed.

'Darling, *I'm* not leaving. I didn't mean to sound as though I was. I just said that you could go if you wanted.'

His romantic expression slowly hardened. 'What are you talking about? We're both going. You can't stay alone. Are you crazy? Either we both stay or we both leave, and you just said—'

'But I'll be home soon. I promise. I'll leave just as soon as the bride's had her first dance with the groom.'

'No! I'm not leaving you here on your own!'

'But why ever not? What harm—?'

'I just don't want to know that you're here with—' He broke off.

His face was chalk-white.

He was staring at the doorway.

Clara turned her tousled blonde head to follow his stare. A very tall old man stood there, the sun on his well-groomed silver hair and elegant grey morning suit. He had great dignity and noble bearing.

'Forgive the intrusion.' His voice had a deep Welsh lilt. 'But I heard voices, see, and thought I ought to warn you. Everybody's sitting down now. The breakfast's about to be served. Thought I'd let you know, so you could come in without a grand entrance.'

The summer breeze lifted strands of black hair from Jared's forehead as he stared. He was utterly silent.

Unmoving. The only clue to his feelings were the chaotic kaleidoscopic lights of his eyes.

'You must be young Jared Blackheath.' The old man stepped forward. 'I'm Owain Llewellyn. Do you remember me?'

Jared released Clara with a swift movement that nearly caught her off balance. 'How do you do?' He strode to Llewellyn, extended his hand, shook the old man's and towered over him like a giant, saying briskly, 'Pleased to meet you. This is my girlfriend, Clara Maye. Clara!'

'Hello!' Clara called shyly, bending to pick up her hat and dust it off while Owain Llewellyn continued to shake Jared's hand with admiration and respect.

'So pleased to meet you,' the old man was saying, a gruff note in his voice as he looked earnestly at Jared. 'So very pleased at last to—'

'Yes, of course.' Jared wrenched his hand away as though burnt, raked long fingers through his hair and looked as though he wanted to be a million miles away.

'How do you do?' Clara rescued him by walking over to shake the old man's hand instead. 'We were just snatching a private moment before the celebrations began.'

'Oh, the celebrations could go on for a very long time.' The bony fingers clasped hers but his old grey eyes were fixed on Jared as he spoke. 'And how lovely that they should begin like this, two young people, so much in love, ready to move into their first home, a home they—'

'I think we should go in,' Jared cut in thickly. His

hand curled around Clara's waist and drew her against him as though she were an amulet to ward off danger. 'Thank you for coming to get us, Mr Llewellyn. I can see the bride sitting down now. It's time we took our places…'

Jared steered them into the dining room without giving the old man a chance to reply. Clara could hardly interfere. It was too late for Jared to leave now, too late for another argument, and they had no choice but to take their places at the top table. Owain Llewellyn was close behind them, sadness in his austere face. As he sat down beside Jared, Clara saw Jared's fist clench on the white tablecloth. She wished she knew why he felt this way.

The wedding breakfast commenced. Jared spoke to Clara continuously throughout the meal. She couldn't believe he'd done it, but he had actually turned his back on poor old Mr Llewellyn, forcing him to eat in isolation at the end of the table. She felt sorry for him. But she also felt a great deal of empathy for Jared. His eyes were still so haunted, and lines of strain were now etched at his mouth as he struggled to keep his feelings hidden from all these people, most of whom were strangers, staring at him because of his fame. He ate almost nothing. He drank far too much champagne. When the meal was over and the speeches began, he turned a whiter shade of pale and Clara frowned at him, not understanding why he should be alarmed by them.

Gareth's father stood up with the microphone. His deep voice boomed around the room. He was quick, witty and entertaining. Even Jared laughed at one or

two jokes. Then the best man stood up and told how
Susie had first met Gareth—mistaking him for a drop-
out because he was asleep on a park bench in torn
jeans, having lost his keys and wallet after a wild
party.

'Gareth was so used to women chasing him for his
money,' said the best man, to ripples of laughter, 'that
he decided to let Susie carry on believing he was a
penniless drop-out. Imagine her shock when she discovered a year later that he was really the heir to the
Llewellyn millions!'

Jared fidgeted restlessly. The best man had finished
his speech and Jared's fingers began scrunching and
unscrunching his napkin with nervous tension.

'And now,' said the best man, 'Owain Llewellyn,
Gareth's grandfather, would like to say a few words.'

The old man got to his feet. Jared was ashen. Clara
suddenly realised what was going to happen. She suddenly remembered Susie saying, 'An old house by the
sea…'

'As you know,' said Owain, 'the Llewellyns are
Welshmen, born and bred. Our headquarters are now
in London, and many of us live here, but we still have
Welsh headquarters, in Cardiff. As many of you
know, my old partner, Daffyd, retired last month,
which leaves the Cardiff offices without a managing
director. There's only one real choice for the post, I'm
sure you'll all agree—my grandson, Gareth.'

Everyone clapped.

'But he needs a home to live in with his new bride.
And I therefore give him my own property, Rhossana
Manor in Rhossana Bay, in the hope that he'll make

it ring with the sounds of love and laughter after so many years of silence.'

And everything fell into place for Clara as she saw Jared's eyes close in defeat.

CHAPTER THREE

TWENTY minutes later Jared walked out of the Ritz. Clara followed, deep in thought. He had not spoken to her since the speech, but then he hadn't had to. She was hardly stupid, and the point had been glaringly obvious. The only reason it had taken her so long to see it was because she'd had such an enormous emotional investment in this wedding right from the start.

All her thoughts and feelings had been focused on Susie: Susie's dress, Susie's guest list, Susie's honeymoon. And Jared's increasing edginess had run along the sidelines. She'd put it down to a fear that she herself would start demanding marriage now that Susie was getting hitched. And perfectly reasonable, too. It had been the logical explanation. Until she'd seen the name on that place setting and thought…does he know this family?

Evidently he did. Whoever the Llewellyns were to Jared, they came from the same little seaside town where Jared had been born, and they clearly pressed on the secret wound he had kept hidden for years. Not just his secret, either. His mother knew about it. So, apparently, did Owain Llewellyn.

What else did Owain know? she wondered. He'd come into the gardens calling Jared 'young Jared Blackheath'. While he was still a dynamic and exciting man, at thirty-seven he could hardly be called 'young', which led Clara to believe that Owain had known Jared when he was a child, living in that lost seaside town of his birth. That wasn't all Owain had said. He'd asked if Jared remembered him, and Clara knew the answer was yes. Jared remembered him only too well. The memory stirred up bitterness and anger, as did the house in Rhossana Bay...

Jared had that haunted look again as he stood at the kerb waiting for Harrison. Hands thrust in trouser pockets, he avoided looking at Clara. To passers-by he was magnificent—a legend, towering indestructibly in the sun. It was only because Clara knew him so well that she was able to see the frayed and frazzled nerves beneath that charismatic exterior.

'We'll be home soon, darling.' She walked to stand beside him.

'Yes...'

'You'll be able to relax then. I'll make you some coffee, massage those tired shoulders.'

'I'll need rather more than that,' he said thickly. Clara's pulses quickened. He was a superb lover at the best and most romantic of times, but after a tense day he was absolutely mind-blowing.

The car flashed up to the kerb. He wrenched open the door to let Clara slide in and a second later was in beside her, closing the door, switching the screen button to give them privacy and closing in on her for a passionate kiss.

It was a way for him to avoid talking. So, for the moment, she let her thoughts slide away as the car swept serenely towards Regent's Park and linked her arms around his strong neck. There was an urgency to his kiss that was breathtaking. He was driven by necessity now.

Her body thrilled in anticipation for the lovemaking to come. All her questions could wait. She'd never forgotten a single detail about this man. That wouldn't change now. He had been the centre of her world since the day she'd first set eyes on him. She remembered the day, the hour, the colour of his tie...

They had met two and a half years ago, at a party in the Grosvenor House Hotel.

Clara had just finished her biggest success in television—an eighteen-month contract on *Ribble Road*—a long-running soap opera set in East London. She'd played Jezebel Whitney, a raven-haired seductress with three lovers, two ex-husbands and a passion for causing trouble. Everyone had hated her. By the time she'd met Jared she had just been murdered. The nation was agog with excitement.

At that time Clara's boyfriend had been another actor in *Ribble Road*. Roger Blake had played one of her lovers, a smooth-talking con-man with blond hair, flashy clothes and an elegant frame. Off-screen he was a likeable young man who had been more of a friend to Clara than anything else. They'd fallen into the habit of seeing each other after a few months and the tabloids had blown the relationship out of all proportion.

Roger had liked being seen out with Clara because she was so instantly recognisable as Jezebel. She'd dyed her hair jet-black for the part, which had meant she had to wear red lipstick and black eyeliner off-screen, because her normal preference for pretty pastels would have looked wrong with all that dark hair.

On the night of her farewell party, however, Clara had dyed her hair back to its natural pale blonde...

Nobody recognised her. Amused, she danced in Roger's arms under the spotlight and murmured, 'Nobody's taking pictures. They must all wonder who I am.'

'Well, why did you dye it back?' Roger was annoyed. 'You're Jezebel. Not Clara. Nobody's interested in Clara. Don't you understand that?'

'I don't want to be Jezebel for the rest of my days! Playing her on screen was fun but it had its drawbacks in real life. I don't like being insulted in the supermarket by well-meaning viewers.'

'You're going to lose all the fame you've just built up, Clara. You should have kept your hair black. Don't you care about your career?'

'I care enough not to get typecast.'

'No danger of that now,' he drawled, and slunk away from her as the music ended.

Shocked, Clara watched him just discard her. He obviously didn't want to know her now that she was no longer the scandalous Jezebel Whitney. And everyone was staring at her now. She felt ridiculous, abandoned in the spotlight. But as she turned to leave the dance floor a strong hand caught her wrist, tugged her gently against a powerful male body. Breathless, she looked up with flashing eyes, about to tell the stranger to get lost. Flashbulbs blinded her. Through a haze she saw blue eyes, a tough, uncompromising face and a firm, sensual mouth.

'Smile!' drawled the deep male voice. 'You're on *Candid Camera*!'

'What do you think you're doing? Stop it!' She was being whirled in his arms, still breathless. 'Who are you?'

'The name's Blackheath. Jared Blackheath.'

'Am I supposed to know you?'

'No, but I want to know you!'

Photographers circled them. Clara racked her brains for his identity. So self-assured and devil-may-care—she was convinced she must have seen him before.

'I've never seen you on set, Mr Blackheath. Are you playing the Inspector, or something?'

'I'd love to play the Inspector with you, Miss Maye.'

She felt herself colour with sudden electrifying excitement.

'Oh...!'

'Oh?' He regarded her with lazy mockery. 'Is that all you can say? Can't you talk without a script?'

'I can talk up a storm, and I can slap your arrogant face, too!'

'Wildcat!' he murmured in her ear. 'But I came here to meet the murdered seductress and instead found a wholesome innocent. Will the real Clara Maye please stand up?'

Fuming, she snapped, 'I'm an actress, Mr Blackheath. That means I'm trained to draw on the darker side of my personality whenever a role calls for it. And we all have a dark side, don't we? I can see from the look in your eyes that you most certainly have one!'

His face darkened instantly and he murmured, 'Clever little thing, aren't you?'

His tone made her shiver as the music ended. They remained in each other's arms. Clara was staring at him as though she had only just seen him.

'Let's sit and have some champagne together,' he said deeply. 'I want to find out what else you can see in my eyes.'

'How about trouble?' she quipped with an excited smile, and he laughed, then led her off the dance floor while the flashbulbs continued to pop all around them. The press were on the scent of their love affair before it had even begun.

He did not leave her side for the rest of the evening.

Next morning three dozen red roses arrived in a silver basket with a note in powerful black handwriting: 'I must see you again. Will tonight be too soon? Blackheath.'

The morning papers arrived and Clara was on the cover of each one. Dancing in Jared Blackheath's arms had made her famous all over again as a blonde. The twist of fate astonished her. Roger rang to congratulate her, but she was very cool and very uninterested. So much for his disloyal belief that she was finished because of the change in her appearance. But who exactly was this gorgeous man who had saved her from obscurity simply by dancing with her? And why did her heartbeat feel so exquisitely unsteady at the thought of seeing him again? Could this be the beginning of true love?

It was.

From then on he bombarded her with calls, visits and kisses. He took her out constantly and conversation flowed like vintage wine between them, so easy and rapid and intimate that she felt there would never be a silence. When silence did come it was so natural, so easy, that she knew their love would last. They became inseparable. His passion was such that she succumbed after only a few weeks. They lived in her bedroom from Saturday night till Wednesday morning, lost in a tidal wave of physical pleasure, coming out only to raid the fridge once every twenty hours when they remembered to eat. When they weren't making love they were holding hands, sitting up till the early hours talking, sharing secrets, unlocking each other emotionally, mentally and then, as the passion rose again, physically.

One night Jared said, 'I want you to move in with me.'

And she replied shyly, 'Just be your live-in lover? But I told you how much I've always wanted to be married...'

'I'm not the marrying kind.' He kissed her, regret in his eyes. 'If I were I would already have proposed to you, because God knows I'm so much in love with you I can't bear to think of life without you.'

Cuddling up, she whispered, 'You'll never have to face life without me, Jared. I've never been in love before. Not like this.'

'Neither have I. I just wish there was some way round the whole marriage showcase.'

'Darling, why do you dislike the idea of it so much?'

'I don't want to be a husband.'

'But why not?'

'I wish I could count the reasons. There are so many. But they all lead to one irrefutable fact: I'll never be a husband. I'll never marry.'

'Is this just fear of commitment, Jared?' she teased.

'If you prefer to think of it as that,' he drawled, 'who am I to stop you?'

But, however much she played it cool, played it light, he wouldn't change his mind. And all he'd ever say was, 'I don't want to be a husband.'

Clara was worried because what she wanted most in the world was a husband. She'd been content to leave that desire on the back burner while she worked for her career. But now that she'd met and fallen so deeply in love with Jared she knew he was The One. Yet it seemed impossible, because he would not countenance the idea of marriage. How could she leave the man she loved just because he wouldn't marry her? So she told herself that he might change his mind after a while. He'd never lived with a woman before—perhaps the experience would make him reassess his feelings about marriage.

So she moved into the white mansion opposite Regent's Park and found herself living a life she'd only dreamt of or acted before. She had realised the day after they met that he was the world-famous businessman-entrepreneur, but she'd had no real conception of what effect that would have on their life-style. She soon found out. It meant private jets, constant international travel, meetings with Heads of State, holidays on private yachts and ceaseless press coverage.

Thankfully, Jared was a more private man than the rest of the world realised. Clara had him all to herself most of the time. Once the front door was closed they lived in their idyllic lovers' paradise, locked away from the rest of the world in happy seclusion and free to be themselves. Of course her own career took her away from him sometimes, but never very far. Television work in London rarely demanded that the actors travel much further than the West End. Elstree was about as far as they got apart from that. And, as most of Clara's work in that first year was in a new and popular sitcom, she fell into a comfortable routine of being driven to and from London studios. It was a light role, but it was work; it kept her in the public eye and it kept her busy—but not too busy. By the time she got in, she always had time to bathe and change before Jared arrived home, so their lives dove-tailed beautifully.

And as they got used to living together so their love deepened, and trust began to really blossom.

'I was brought up in a tiny Welsh village,' Jared told her after they'd been living together for three months. 'With no money, no prospects and parents who argued constantly.'

'Is that why you dislike the idea of marriage?'

'Probably. Plus, of course, I was an only child. Both my parents tried to use me to win whatever argument was going on. The house was so small I couldn't escape. All I heard all day was shouting, shouting and more shouting. I used to go and hide in the coal shed just to escape the noise.'

Clara let him talk, rarely stopping him with a question. But he always found a way to change the subject if he found himself telling her too much too soon. Information came at a slow pace and she cherished every snippet.

Then one day he said out of the blue, 'My mother's arriving in London next weekend.'

Clara nearly dropped the cup in her hand. 'But I thought both your parents were dead!'

'Can't think why,' he said, avoiding her eyes.

Staring, she asked, 'Have you heard from your mother since I've been living here? I don't remember it at all. Not even a mention. And I've been here six months.'

'My father died when I was eight, but my mother's still very much alive. She lives in a house which I bought for her a few years back.'

She asked carefully, 'How did your father die?'

'In a fall.' His voice was casual yet he turned his back, but not before she had seen the darkness flare in his eyes with a bitter bedrock power that made her instincts buzz.

'And you lived with your mother after that?'

'Yes,' he said, and changed the subject.

After that it became clear that his mother always stayed at the Dorchester when she came on her rare visits to London, that although Jared paid all her expenses, took her on fabulous shopping trips and dined out at top restaurants with her, his mother never stayed at the white mansion in Regent's Park. Never. It was as though he could only tolerate her on neutral ground.

Clara couldn't understand it. Lily Blackheath seemed a perfectly nice woman in her late fifties, well-groomed and elegant with once-dazzling blue eyes like her son's. And they never talked about Wales. In fact, Jared rarely mentioned Wales. He occasionally told her about his school, his adolescent street-fights in Cardiff and his first experience of women…but he rarely mentioned his home life. The subject of his parents was one he shied away from. And she quickly learnt not to pry. He gave monosyllabic answers at best—stony silence at worst.

But they were in love. They were happy. And Clara was content to let the mysteries he kept from her remain his own private province…

Or she had been until now, Clara thought, Now, as the limousine pulled up at the gates of their Regent's Park home, Clara had a strong feeling that all those mysteries were about to open up. Their passionate kiss in the back of the car ended. Sitting back, Jared breathed hard while Clara tidied her hair. They slid up a small tree-lined drive to the white pillars of the front entrance. Although stately, the house had ivy climbing the front redbrick wall and a bright blue front door which seemed to smile in welcome whenever they returned home.

'We'll go straight up to bed,' Jared murmured.

'Yes, darling.' She wasn't going to argue with that!

They held hands as they stepped out of the car to walk up the white steps and through the open double doors.

A magnificent hallway greeted them. Sunlight shone from a glass dome above. It lit up the balustrade staircase to a brilliant white, with the smooth black and white marble floor and the palms which flourished in terracotta pots adding a splash of colour to an otherwise imposing hall.

Mrs Harrison, the housekeeper, was waiting for them. A small, plump woman with a Somerset accent, she wore her usual floral frock and pinny while her salt-and-pepper hair escaped from an untidy bun.

'Good afternoon sir, madam. Shall I make tea?'

'Thank you, Mrs Harrison,' Jared said with winning charm, 'but we'll be going upstairs. I have a headache and Clara is rather tired. That's why we came home so early. We'll be going straight upstairs to lie down for a while. If we want anything later, we'll ring down.'

'Very good, sir.'

Their hands were linked as they went up the red-carpeted stairs. A chandelier winked at them. They turned onto the upstairs corridor, also carpeted in red.

'I really do have a headache, you know,' he confided.

'I know the best cure for that...'

'Yes...' He pushed open the master bedroom door and took her in his arms. 'Oh, darling, you can't imagine how much I want you...'

His kiss was tender. As her fingers slid along his neck and into his dark hair she felt the tension which had built up during the reception and began to massage his neck. He groaned against her mouth. His hands moved to the zip of her dress. He gently pulled it down with a smooth movement and she shivered as it fell in a pool of cream silk luxury around her high-heeled shoes.

Passion flared between them. Breathing hard together, they clung to one another. Jared groaned again as Clara fumbled with his tie, the buttons of his shirt, shaking with desire as she began to undress him and he her. He unclipped her silk bra. Her breasts were freed and in his hands, pink nipples springing erect with excitement as he bent his dark head to suck greedily until she was trembling with need, clutching his dark head and whispering his name.

Suddenly he scooped her into his arms, carried her to the bed and stared down at her with feverish eyes, breathing hard as though he couldn't wait any longer, his body hard already and pulsing with hot blood as he slid on top of her on the bed.

'I love you!' she whispered.

Kissing her deeply, he finished unbuttoning his waistcoat and shirt, shrugging them off without taking his mouth from hers, and when he was bare-chested she ran her hands hungrily over his hard-muscled, dark-haired chest. Her long, stockinged thighs slid apart for him. She felt free, wanton. Her tongue slid against his and she moaned as his hands moved up her spread thighs to caress her buttocks tantalisingly before sliding her cream silk briefs slowly down, very slowly down.

Oh... Her legs slid open again for him and the

blood pulsed round her body so fast she could feel it drumming through her skin. She kissed him fiercely. And, though his need was harder, more urgent, he didn't lose control. His fingers trailed up lightly between her thighs. His heartbeat slammed at his chest yet still he kept her waiting, made her want him more, until she began to fumble with his trousers, sliding the zip down as her skin grew warm with sweat.

Naked, too, his powerful body slid against hers in the lovemaking dance. Clara moaned so deeply that his breath caught with excitement. Still he kept control, although she could feel the enormity of his excitement, and she begged him now.

He delighted her with a long harsh cry of need, then kissed her deeper, saying her name over and over as he moved inexorably to take her...

For a minute or two afterwards they lay in silence, listening to the blood roaring through their joined bodies. Everything gradually returned to normal. Clara stroked his damp head, kissed the pulse that still throbbed in his neck. His whole body was relaxed now. The strain of the day must have been terrible for him. She was glad to have helped him relinquish it. Set his burden down. Get rid of it, if only briefly in her arms.

Suddenly he raised his head, still breathing hard, and smiled down at her. 'My God, I needed that!'

She laughed. 'So did I! But not, I agree...' her eyes saddened '...as much as you did.'

He lowered his gaze. 'Everything was just so difficult today. I did my best to stay cool and collected. But somehow it never really swung into first gear.'

'And you're normally so completely in control of every situation. That's why I'd give almost anything to know precisely why you were so ruffled by the Llewellyn family. Most notably, Owain Llewellyn Senior.'

He was silent and still. Then he shifted, withdrew from her body and slid away, taking his loving warmth with him. She watched him anxiously. He was usually so loving after making love with her. For him to withdraw so silently was not only upsetting but completely out of character.

'I don't want to talk about it,' he said, and got off the bed, blundering away to the bathroom as though he couldn't see properly.

Clara sat up. The door slammed behind him. Something was very wrong. He was playing for time in there, apart from anything. She could hear him moving about, fiddling with aftershave bottles, washing his hands and generally pretending to have a busy time. He was hoping she'd forget about the very real and important questions burning in her mind. Hoping she'd drop the subject by the time he came out. But she couldn't do that.

His secret had always been there, waiting in the wings to make its grand entrance and overturn their happy life together. There was no point in pretending it would go away. Not now. It had been spectacularly ushered to centre stage by the appearance in both their lives of the Llewellyn family. Susie had just married into them and Susie was not going to go away. How, therefore, could the problem of the Llewellyns be resolved?

Suddenly the bathroom door clicked open. Jared emerged. He had put on his dark red dressing gown. His face was wary. His eyes were very dark as he looked at her.

'Darling,' she said softly, 'do come back to bed. I want to talk, and it's much easier with your arms around me.'

'What do you want to talk about?'

'Well...Susie is a Llewellyn now.'

He walked immediately to the windows. He looked out, hands thrust in the pockets of his robe, and said nothing. He was good at this. Avoiding questions with silence was one of his favourite tactics. Or just giving clever political replies. Or sometimes even plain side-stepping them. All businessmen were good at these things, and Jared was a king among businessmen. He was hardly going to drop his tactics and spill the beans at the first difficult question about the Llewellyns.

'Susie is a Llewellyn now, Jared,' Clara repeated bluntly. 'I know you don't want her to be, but she is.'

'I never said I didn't want her to be.' He traced imaginary dust on the window ledge.

'Well, that's the way it seems to me. And if the Llewellyns can rattle you the way they did today it might present a problem for the future.'

'Possibly.'

'Susie wants children.'

He raked a hand through his hair.

'Lots of them. I promised her years ago, back in the orphanage, that I'd be godmother when she—'

'Yes, all right,' he muttered thickly. 'I see your point!'

'Do you, darling?' Her worried eyes scanned his profile. 'If you really mean that, perhaps you could answer a few questions for me.'

His mouth tightened. 'Very well. Get on with it.'

'Well…' She clasped her arms around her knees, the sheet covering her bare legs. 'I think I'm right in believing that Owain Llewellyn is the main reason for your behaviour today. I didn't notice him at the wedding ceremony. I don't think I even noticed him when the photos were being taken. But I realise in retrospect that his presence is what upset you more than anything else about that wedding.'

He gave a harsh sigh and said nothing.

'That's why you started flirting with the brunette, isn't it? To divert attention from the photos and possibly even to get out of having them taken.'

'I flirted with her because I was on edge,' he said curtly. 'It's that simple. I wanted your attention. I wanted you to come home with me. I wanted to leave.'

'I see…'

He gave a rough sigh, turned to look at her. 'I'm sorry. I shouldn't have done it. It's the first time I've ever flirted with another woman since I met you.'

'I know, darling. And of course I forgive you. Now that I realise what kind of strain you were really under, I understand precisely why you did it. But I need to know why you were under that strain in the first place.'

He was ominously silent.

'Jared, we've lived together without ever delving into your past overmuch. But I don't think we can do that any more. I think fate took it out of our hands the day Susie fell in love with Gareth Llewellyn, and now all we can do is accept it, deal with it and find a way to live with her choice of husband.'

He turned from her. He rapped long fingers on the windowsill. Early evening sunlight slanted in across his tough face, turning it deep gold where his tan absorbed the light.

'Did you know he'd given them the house in Rhossana Bay?'

He waited a long time, then said deeply, 'I wasn't sure. But I suspected.'

'Would I be wrong in thinking that the house represents something to you? Something connected with Owain Llewellyn? Something that might have a connection with your childhood? Your parents?'

He placed both hands on the windowsill, leaning against it as though standing at his desk after a difficult business meeting, trying to weigh up the balance and come to a decision which would affect the hundreds of people working for a company he was about to take over...only this wasn't a company. This was him.

Slowly, Clara got off the bed. Barefoot, she walked softly to him, scooping up his white shirt on the way and shouldering into it. It hung loose on her petite frame.

'Jared...?' she asked as gently as she could. 'Did Owain Llewellyn know your parents in Rhossana Bay?'

He studied the distant sunlit trees of the park. 'Yes…yes, we all knew Owain Llewellyn back in those days. Back in Rhossana Bay…'

CHAPTER FOUR

'HE WAS like the local squire to us. There were fêtes in the grounds of the Manor, charity lunches, cocktail parties and even the occasional ball in the Great Ballroom. What a beautiful old room that was. What a beautiful manor. Everybody knew him. Everybody loved him. Everybody including me and…both my parents.'

'Did something happen to change all this?'

His dark lashes flickered. 'My mother had an affair with him.'

Of all the punchlines in all the world, that was the very last she'd expected to hear. Lily Blackheath and Owain Llewellyn. They moved together in her mind to form the second big picture in the jigsaw puzzle of Jared's secret. And now that she could see them together it seemed right, somehow, for they made a distinguished couple. The age-gap could only have been about seven or eight years—no greater than that between herself and Jared. They both had strong personalities, and an inexplicable sadness in their eyes.

'I was eight when the affair became public knowledge,' Jared continued after a pause. 'I shouldn't remember that much about it, but I do. I remember every last detail. The way my mother was always finding excuses to go to the Manor. The glib explanations she handed my father whenever gossip filtered

through to him. The whispers and stares in the street.
And, of course, the way my schoolfriends mocked me.
They didn't dare bully me because I fought back too
furiously to make it worth their while. They were
scared stiff of me. But there are other ways to kick a
boy in the teeth without even moving your foot.' His
smile was cynical, yet somehow accepting. 'They
sniggered and whispered whenever I was around. So
did the rest of the village. It was an open secret and
I was a sitting duck.'

Clara's voice was husky with compassion but she
knew she must not show too much, for his pride was
as strong as his dignity. 'When did your father find
out about the affair?'

'Not for some time. He tried to close his ears and
eyes, the way most cuckolded husbands do. And he
had good reason to do so. He worked for Llewellyn.
He could hardly go round to the Manor and punch his
boss on the nose. So he blanked it all out until it
became intolerable. That's when the rows really took
off at home.'

'Do you think it was just a temporary fling for your
mother?'

'Oh, no, she was in love with Owain.' He shot her
a grim look. 'No matter how much I hate the pair of
them for what they did, I've never doubted the
strength of their love.'

'Does that make it harder to talk about it?'

'It makes me feel hurt for my father, Clara.' Pain
shone in his eyes. He'd never spoken about his father
to her. Nor shown her a photograph of him. She knew

nothing about him except that he had died when Jared was eight. She didn't even know his name.

Treading more carefully, she asked, 'Did your father still love Lily while all this was going on?'

'Yes,' he said thickly, with absolute conviction, and then refused to add to that statement.

After a second, she asked, 'But she didn't love him?'

'In retrospect, I don't think it would be fair to speculate on that. It's probably too complicated. They were teenagers when they met. They got married when they were nineteen. Too young, really. They were parents a year later, at the age of twenty, and by the time I was seven years old my mother had had enough of being a dutiful housewife and mother. She'd become a very different person from the girl my father married. I think by the time the affair started the rows had been going on for some time regardless. Of course they got much, much worse as the affair progressed. But they were already symptomatic of the final stages of their marriage. In the end, there was a row to end all rows and my mother walked out.'

'She walked out…?'

'Wham. Just like that. Left us both.'

'But where did she go?'

'To the Manor.'

Her breath caught.

'To Owain Llewellyn,' he finished, with a cold hard smile, and then turned to look out of the window again, his eyes brooding.

Clara somehow managed not to speak until she'd

had time to assimilate this latest piece of the jigsaw. No wonder he'd tried to avoid the wedding. No wonder he'd been alarmed by the seating arrangements. And how completely understandable his horror over the wedding speech seemed now. For Jared to realise—who knew how long ago?—that Owain would give the Manor to Gareth and Susie as a wedding present, right in front of him, must have been a nightmare he'd been fighting to avoid ever since the couple met.

Clara pressed on, sure now that she was only looking at the first pieces of the puzzle. 'And then what happened? Is that when your father came to—?'

'Let's go back to bed.' He turned suddenly to smile at her, but his smile was tense and she knew he wanted to close the subject before she found out too much. 'All this talk of the past is giving me another headache.'

'But, darling—'

'How many times must I tell you?' His face hardened with temper. 'I don't want to talk about this!'

'Jared, we need to if—'

'Dwelling on the past is a waste of time and thoroughly unpleasant into the bargain. Now come on! Bed!' His tone brooked no argument as he took her wrist, leading her along with him towards the bed. 'Or I'll put you over my knee and teach you what happens to girls who ask too many questions!'

Clara laughed breathlessly as he threw her onto the bed. He was very sexy again, and her heart beat with excitement as he moved with a look of dark intent in his eyes. Apart from the fact that it was best to let the subject slide, she knew she had no intention of missing out on some more of his wonderful lovemaking.

'Oh, darling...!' she whispered unsteadily as her arms went around his neck. She tossed all questions out of her mind and lay back...

Some time in the night she was woken by Jared moving fitfully in his sleep. Blinking tiredly and letting her eyes adjust to the darkness, she remembered their passionate lovemaking, and then realised Jared was twisting in the grip of a terrible nightmare.

'No!' he kept saying as his body thrashed from side to side. 'No...'

Clara sat up. Should she wake him? She wasn't sure if it was dangerous or not.

'Still there...can't be!' His voice grew hoarse. 'Da...Da, wake up!'

Da? she thought, perplexed. But he was obviously trying to wake himself up, or why was he talking about waking?

'Come down! Come back!'

And then he shattered her belief that she really knew him.

He broke into fluent Welsh, and then, 'He's dead and you killed him!' Then shot bolt-upright in bed, drenched in cold sweat as his breath came in fierce gasps and his heart hammered like a galloping horse.

'It's all right.' Clara put her arms around him loosely, not wanting to constrict him with a close embrace when he was still disorientated. 'It was only a dream. You're safe now. I'm here.'

'Just a dream...' He sounded deeply relieved as he

stared into the darkness, put a hand to his forehead, eyes closing. 'Just a dream…only a dream…'

She waited while he calmed down but knew he might forget the dream if she waited too long. He put his arms round her and breathed a deep sigh of relief. She felt him relax and said quickly, 'What was the dream about? Tell me what you can remember. You kept calling out something I didn't understand. Something like ''Da—'''

'I don't know what you're talking about,' he interrupted as he tensed. 'I can't even remember the dream. Just a load of nonsense.'

'You were talking in Welsh, too. I didn't know you spoke Welsh.'

'Neither did I,' he drawled in that fake upper class English accent. 'It was probably your imagination. As for the dream, I can guess what brought that on. Hunger! Do you realise it's gone midnight and I haven't eaten for forty-eight hours? I barely touched the wedding breakfast and didn't eat a thing yesterday! I'm so hungry I could eat a rhinocerous!'

She looked into his guarded, smiling face and knew he was lying. He remembered the dream all right. Just as he knew who Da was. And that he spoke fluent Welsh, but she'd have to leave the questions for now…

'I bet Mrs H is asleep.' He was still faintly breathless but putting on a dazzling show of nonchalance. 'I wonder who'll cook me something nice to eat!'

Smiling in spite of herself, she said, 'I just wonder!'

They tiptoed downstairs hand in hand. The house was silent save for the quarter-hour chime of the grandfather clock. Mr and Mrs Harrison were fast asleep, which left them free to make themselves at home in the kitchen.

Jared inspected the contents of the fridge.

'Hmm! I think I fancy smoked salmon and scrambled eggs on toast. You're very good at that, darling. I love the way you make the eggs. Every bit as good as the Ritz!'

'Not trying to butter me up, are you?'

He grinned. The kitchen was very big, well furnished and built in a wide square with pine-fronted cupboards. In the centre stood the vast cooking area. Copper pots and pans hung from the walls. There was a raised level at one end which held a pine table and chairs for the staff to eat at. Jared liked eating there too. It reminded him of simpler times, when he hadn't been a multi-millionaire with a dining room the size of a ballroom. He also loved to sit alone with Clara and watch her cook. Men were such funny creatures.

'How many eggs?' Clara asked when she'd put butter in the saucepan and was busy breaking eggs into a cup.

'Just six.'

She laughed.

'Oh—and I'll have all the smoked salmon, too.'

'Ziggy-piggy!'

He came up behind her, slid his arms around her waist and kissed her neck. She laughed again, enjoying his light humour. If he preferred to forget about his nightmare it would be stupid and unfair of her to try to stop him. He'd had a terrible time of it with the wedding. He deserved a break, the chance to relax, be himself and have fun.

A cat mewed outside the back door. They both turned to stare in the direction of the plaintive cry. Unblinking emerald eyes peered at them from the sheer blackness of the glass door and seemed to envy their cosy bright-lit love.

'A black cat.' Clara smiled. 'Oh, that's good luck.'

'Sure is.' Jared strolled to the back door. 'Maybe Owain Llewellyn will turn into a toad next week and I'll never have to sit next to him again. Or maybe I'll get this wine deal in California and make another couple of million quid. Just in case, I shall give Kitty a saucer of milk…' But when he opened the back door the cat sprang away. He went out in search of it, leaving Clara to put the toast on, cut the smoked salmon into thin strips the way he liked it and put the kettle on for some decaffeinated coffee.

By the time he returned she was just putting the finishing touch of a sprig of parsley on top of his mountain of scrambled eggs.

'Couldn't catch Kitty. So I got you a present instead.' He produced a single red rose from behind his back.

Touched, she said huskily, 'Darling…'

'I got pricked by a thorn because it was so dark.' He presented his finger for inspection.

Clara kissed it better, but within seconds he had pulled her into his arms and held her there in silence for a long moment, unmoving. Listening to his heartbeat, she thought again of the nightmare. He almost never had bad dreams. He usually slept like a log.

Still, she didn't have to look far to see the cause of the nightmare…

'Your food's getting cold,' she said softly after a moment.

'Oh, yes…' He released her with a kiss, avoiding her eyes, and she knew there was pain in there but that he wouldn't show it. A woman had to be a mind-reader in order to love a man. Or was it an emotion-reader? Probably both, but that was what made the world go round, and maybe she wouldn't have it any other way.

They moved to the kitchen table to sit together on the pine chairs. He ate hungrily while she nibbled at a slice of toast with low-fat spread on it.

'Dieting again?' Jared asked after consuming most of his egg mountain.

'I've got to, just in case I'm called for the test. Mitch thinks there's a strong chance I'll get the part of Rachel.'

'You've been rehearsing the script for weeks, though.'

'Night and day,' she groaned. 'But it's such a wonderful part. A starring role in a powerful drama series. I even get three monologues. Lots of sincerity, passion and even some serious crying to do in episode four!'

He studied her with a sudden gleam in his eyes and observed slowly, 'That kind of stuff could win you an award, Clara.'

'Or at the very least a nomination.' She blushed at her own high hopes.

'What a talented girlfriend I have. By far the most

versatile actress in the business, too, in my opinion.'
He smiled at her, then reached for her hand across the
table, squeezed it lightly. 'I'm proud of you, baby.'

'Darling…' She felt tears of love in her eyes. 'I
don't know what I'd do without you. I had to fight so
hard for the confidence I now have as an actress.
People told me so many times that I'd never make
anything of myself but I wouldn't listen. I couldn't
let myself listen. It was too important to me to *be*
somebody.'

'That's how we all get there. The fuel of the driven
few is just the need for recognition. I saw it in you
the night we met.'

'I thought you wanted to meet Jezebel Whitney that
night!'

'I did, but I knew as soon as I saw you that I was
going to fall in love.' He studied her honest face. 'I
move in such a corrupt world. It's tough at the top,
and what makes it tough is having no one to trust. I
guess I'd reached the end of the line when I met you.
I couldn't stand it any longer. I had to trust someone.
I needed you, Clara.' His voice deepened. 'I still do.'

Their fingers linked tenderly across the table.
'Sometimes I wonder if you really do trust me, Jared.
It upsets me to know how long you suffered in silence
about this wedding.'

'I don't have to keep silent any longer, though—
do I?' He tugged at her hand so that she half-stood
half-slid onto his lap. Pushing his plate away, he
cradled her on his lap, kissing her mouth. 'Thanks
to you. The persistent and perceptive Miss
Clara Maye…'

'You haven't told me everything, though, have you, Jared?' she asked softly.

His eyes became guarded. 'I've told you the truth.'

'About everything?'

He answered with a kiss and she allowed herself to be silenced. But as she gave herself up to his love she knew her silence would not—could not—last long.

He left for Texas on Monday morning. Clara saw him to the door in her ivory satin dressing gown. Cool sunlight mingled at the open front doors with the scent of the exhaust fumes and the sound of birds singing in the park as Harrison waited discreetly in the Rolls, engine running.

'I'll call you every day,' Jared said, as he always did when going away. 'I wish you could come with me. Can't Mitch give you a definite date for this test yet?'

'You know what it's like in television. Everything's up in the air, dates get shifted, programmes are cancelled at a moment's notice... I have to be on the spot or I could miss it altogether.'

'Oh, well,' he said with an arrogant look. 'I'll just have to boast about you and content myself with long late-night phone calls.'

Wrapping herself around him, she buried her face in his dark cashmere coat and breathed in the scent of his skin, his aftershave. 'I'll miss you terribly.'

'I'll be back before you know it.' There was a pause before he spoke in a wary voice without looking at her. 'When do Gareth and Susie get back from their honeymoon?'

'A fortnight. They should get back just before you fly home from California.'

He nodded, but as he drew back she saw his eyes—those hard black pupils and the ever-shifting shards of blue glittering like shrapnel in the kaleidoscope she knew so well.

After she had waved goodbye she stood there for a long moment, shivering slightly, deep in thought. She had a feeling their lives were moving towards some crisis point. And, no matter how much she told herself not to be ridiculous, it was a feeling she could not shake...

Time passed slowly, as it always did when he was away. But he rang every night and they spoke for an hour or two while she lay in bed, a cup of peach and passion-fruit tea beside her, gazing at the smiling photograph of him which stood framed in gold on her bedside table.

'How's it going?' she would ask.

'Brilliantly,' he would say, with his usual charming arrogance. 'How do you think?'

But he wasn't always arrogant.

'Any news from Susie and Gareth?' he always asked, with that wary edge to his voice.

And she always replied, 'They're on their honeymoon, darling. They probably won't even get out of bed, let alone start writing postcards or ringing old friends.'

He obviously wanted to know the minute they returned. Clara made a note of it. She would ring Susie just as soon as she thought they might be back so that

Jared could know what was going on. Anything to put his mind at rest.

Mitch finally rang about the test ten days after Jared had left. He was in an energetic panic because the test had been rush-arranged at the last minute. Clara wasn't thrown by the panic. She was exhilarated by it. It was the waiting that had unnerved her.

On the next day, the day itself, she went to the studios, went through Hair and Make-up and arrived on the soundstage to find familiar cameras, cables and an encouraging director.

As the cameras rolled she was already Rachel. She began the monologue, using all her skills, building slowly from a low voice, emphasising powerful words and letting her voice break on others. She drew breath with a tremor before shouting, and turned her face away with pained eyes to whisper the next line. Then she was free to build again until she reached the climax with shattering emotional power.

When she finished there was a hushed silence. She was shaking with the force of emotion unleashed.

'Yes,' said the director, and she heard the smile in his voice.

Later, she met Mitch for a drink at the Sloane Grill. They sat on the pavement in the early evening sun, watching expensively dressed women late-night shopping at the exclusive designer shops. Clara wondered why some of the women spent a fortune on couture clothes when a pair of faded jeans and a white top could make any woman as slim as they were look far more lovely and natural.

'I think you've got it,' Mitch told her as he ate his

Caesar Salad. 'I've never heard such an enthusiastic "We'll be in touch." Not even when you landed Jezebel Whit—'

'That name will follow me to the grave,' she groaned. 'Playing Rachel is the only way I'll ever supercede Jezebel and leave her behind for ever.'

'You met Jared through Jezebel. Don't knock it.'

Clara laughed. They'd been together as agent and actress for eight years now.

A good-looking, slender man, Mitch was fastidious about his appearance: thick dark hair was always perfectly blow-dried in the latest cut, and his immaculate clothes were the last word in elegance and style. And he had a personality that was sheer showbiz. Mitch could razzle-dazzle better than most of his artistes, and consequently ran one of the most successful agencies in town.

When she arrived home at eight o'clock the phone was ringing.

'Where've you been?' Jared's dark voice demanded. 'I've been ringing for hours but—'

'It's Mrs H's day off.' She was breathless, leaning over to kick the front door shut. 'And I just spent the day at the television studios doing my test…'

They talked for some time and Jared was delighted to hear she'd done well. But when she put the phone down she remembered only the worried note in his voice and knew it was because of Susie, Gareth and the house in Rhossana Bay.

Next day she was still worrying about it. So she rang Susie's London flat to see if they were back yet.

'Yes, we got back last night.' Susie yawned

sleepily. 'I'm jet lagged to death and my new husband is being a bit grumpy.'

'No, I'm not!' yelled Gareth in the background.

Susie giggled. 'Husbands! Honestly—what can you do with them?'

Clara's heart ached with sadness, knowing Jared might never marry her, that she might never have the husband she wanted and loved. But she checked the feelings. She wasn't going to be driven to envy her friend's happiness. She was happy for Susie. If a little sad sometimes for herself.

'Did you have a super-romantic time?' she asked lovingly.

'Super-dreamy. But we don't have time to dwell on it. I'm up to my ears in unpacking and repacking. Gareth wants to move to Wales right away. We're driving down to Rhossana Bay this afternoon.'

It was the last thing Clara wanted to hear.

After a great deal of thought, she decided not to disturb Jared with the news. It would only upset him. And there was nothing he could do about it. Rhossana Bay was now Gareth and Susie's home town and that was that. When Jared called that night she told him just that Gareth and Susie were back and would be moving to Rhossana Bay as soon as possible. She also promised that she would not, under any circumstances, visit the little seaside town without Jared's knowledge or consent.

She broke that promise within forty-eight hours.

'Miss Clara!' Mrs Harrison's voice sailed up the stairs on Monday morning. 'Telephone for you! Shall I transfer it to your bedroom?'

'Yes, please! Number seven!' Clara put her body lotion down, tugged on a silk robe and padded barefoot to the bed as the extension rang. She snatched it up, thinking it would be Jared because he was expected home tonight. 'Hello…?'

'Miss Maye?'

The unfamiliar voice made her tense. 'Speaking…'

'Owain Llewellyn, here. I don't know if you remember me, but—'

'Of course I remember you.' Her voice was unsteady. A sudden premonition made her skin flush hot, then icy cold. 'How are you? What can I do for you?'

'I'm afraid this isn't a social call, Miss Maye, much as I would prefer it to be. I have bad news.' His gruff Welsh voice alarmed her. 'There's been an accident…'

'Susie!' Clara sank breathless onto the bed, groping for calm as her stomach plummeted. 'She's not dead! Please tell me she's—'

'She's still alive.'

'Oh, thank God!'

'But she's in a coma.'

'Oh, no…no…' she whispered, as she put her hand to her mouth.

'Apparently she decided to take a stroll along the cliffs behind the Manor. She's a city girl. She lost her footing, slipped and fell down the cliff and into the sea.'

'How badly is she hurt?'

'Quite badly—she's fractured her skull.'

'Oh, my God...' She was whispering like a broken record.

'Her injuries aren't as bad as they could have been. A fall like that would have killed most people. It's because she's so fit, see. The doctors believe she rolled with the fall and the strength of her muscles protected most of her bones.'

'All those aerobics classes!' Clara laughed tearfully, and realised she was in a state of shock as the tears rolled down her cheeks.

'At any rate—the coma is serious and we need your help. Gareth is with her now. The doctors say it'll help if people she loves talk to her. Apparently people can hear things even though they're in a coma. Gareth insisted I rang you. He believes the combination of the two of you will help keep her alive and maybe even wake her up eventually.'

Clara didn't hesitate. 'Where is she?'

He gave her the address of the hospital and she told him she'd drive down directly. As soon as she put the phone down she picked it up again and rang San Francisco.

But Jared was working late into the night, flying over the Napa Valley with the MD of his vineyard, Blackheath Californian Wines. With the best will in the world nobody could get a message to him.

Clara knew he'd be pole-axed when he discovered that not only had she gone to Wales but also that Susie was in danger.

She left a message which would not alarm him in front of his staff. He knew her well enough to know it was urgent. Then she rang Mitch to tell him she was leaving town.

'Oh, poor Susie!' Mitch was saddened by the news. 'Why do these things always happen to the nicest people? Life's so unfair.'

Clara couldn't agree more.

Summoning the Harrisons, she explained the situation, giving Mrs Harrison strict instructions to tell Jared where she'd gone, why she'd gone and how he could contact her direct.

Then she went upstairs, packed a large suitcase and left for Susie, for Wales, for Rhossana.

CHAPTER FIVE

SUSIE was alone in a glass room. Broken and battered, she lay swathed in bandages around her head, arm and both her legs. Nurses watched her constantly, both inside the glass room and outside, sitting on a central podium from which they could see everything.

Clara burst into tears as soon as she saw her. Hearing about the accident was one thing. The reality was quite another. Sobbing, she walked to the bed where Gareth sat in a desperate vigil.

'Thank God you're here.' Gareth was ashen-faced. A very different man from the smiling young groom of two weeks ago. 'I couldn't think of anyone else who might be able to help. My own family have been wonderful, of course, but they barely know Susie and the doctors don't believe she'll respond to them. But I know she'll respond to you.'

'I hope so.' Clara sank onto the chair beside him. Staring at Susie, she flinched at the face, half-hidden by bandages. Her mouth was cut, bruised and swollen. 'Has there been any change in her?'

'Nothing. No response at all.'

'And her injuries?'

'A fractured collarbone. Two broken ribs. Three broken fingers. A broken arm. A broken leg...' The list went on to include lesions and cuts.

Trying not to sound as shaken as she felt, Clara said, 'And the doctors say we should just talk to her?'

'That's it. Just keep on talking. One day she might hear us and wake up.' His face crumpled and he started to cry. Clara put her arm around him and held him until the crying subsided.

Gently, she said, 'Why don't you take a break? The nurses tell me there's a coffee machine in the waiting room, and they sell sandwiches at the shop. I'll take over until you feel stronger.'

'What if she dies while I'm away?'

Her blood ran cold. 'I won't let her die. Believe me—I need her just as much as you do.'

With a trembling smile he went out to take his break. Clara linked her fingers with the hand of Susie's that was not damaged. It was warm and limp. She started to talk. Time slipped by. Gareth returned, much stronger and able to talk with her. Night fell. Midnight came and went. Still they talked.

Clara took a break at three a.m. She'd had no sleep since Sunday night. It was now Tuesday morning and she was so tired she could barely think, kept bumping into things. But a tuna sandwich and a coffee made her feel much better. She asked at Reception if there'd been a telephone call from Jared, but there hadn't. Worried and upset, she considered ringing London to find out if Mrs H had heard from him. The payphone at the hospital took credit cards. But it was three-thirty a.m. by that time, and too late to ring. Returning to the glass room, she took up her vigil with Gareth.

'Still here?' A voice said from the doorway at eight in the morning.

Exhausted, Clara turned red eyes to see Owain
Llewellyn. He looked for a second as Jared had described him: gone was the old man from the wedding
and in his place stood a powerful silhouette of a man
with dazzling grey eyes and an air of charismatic
strength. Then he stepped closer. Suddenly he was
silver-haired and sixty again, but the illusion had been
strong enough to let Clara see how very attractive he
had once been—and still was for a man of his age.

'Grandpa...' Gareth rubbed tired eyes. 'It's not
working. We've talked all night but—'

'Don't expect miracles,' Owain said gently. 'And
don't push yourself too hard. Look at you. I bet you
haven't eaten or slept since the accident.'

Gareth looked vague. 'I had a sandwich yesterday.'

'Well, you won't do Susie any good by exhausting
yourself— either of you. I've come to make sure you
get proper food and rest. Gareth—you're to go home
at once. The same goes for you, Miss Maye. A room
has been made up for you at the Manor. I want—'

'No.' She got unsteadily to her feet, wilting now
with lack of sleep but determined to be loyal to Jared.
'I'll be staying at a hotel. Not at the Manor.'

'May I ask which hotel—so I can keep you in-
formed about Susie?'

'I haven't booked it yet. I'll go and do that now.'

'But it's the height of the holiday season! You'll
be lucky to get a room between here and Cardiff!'

He was right. Clara spent an hour on the payphone,
trying to get a room with no success. Every hotel, bed
and breakfast and even the local inns were full for

miles around. The tourist board couldn't come up with
a solution and neither could Clara.

On the edge of tears with hysteria and exhaustion,
Clara realised she had no option but to go to the
Manor. Her nerves were close to breaking point.
Sticking to her diet had already depleted her energy
levels, to say nothing of her blood sugar. And poor
old faithful Harrison was in a terrible state after a
difficult night on the waiting room couch in his chauffeur's uniform, now crumpled and unsightly.

With a heavy heart Clara swallowed her pride and
tried to forget her fear about how Jared would feel
when he found out—and accepted the room at the
Manor.

A crumbling old mansion, it stood close to the cliffs
with the sea glittering witch-green behind its sloping
Welsh walls. Yellowing paint peeled on every
wooden surface.

'Looks a bit like a ghost house to me,' commented
Harrison. 'You sure it's the right place?'

'It said Rhossana Manor on the gates.'

As they stopped by the front door it opened and
Gareth came out. Harrison brought the cases from the
boot while Clara went to the steps.

'Your rooms have been made up,' Gareth told them
with a heavy yawn and quick ruffle of his untidy hair.
'I'll show you where to go. Excuse the mess. This
place is in a terrible state.'

They followed him into the house in fascinated silence.

A musty smell immediately overwhelmed them.

Dust sheets still covered some of the furniture in the hall. The whole place echoed with their footsteps and voices.

Shocked, Clara said, 'I thought you moved in a few days ago? Is the whole house like this?'

'No, several rooms have been refurbished. Four of the bedrooms, three of the bathrooms, the dining and drawing rooms...'

'How many rooms are there in all?'

'About forty.' He smiled as he went up the stairs. 'It's been like this for ages, you know. Thirty years, to be precise. Boarded up, covered in dust—that's why Grandpa wanted us to have it. He'd already secretly started renovating it but Susie and I tied the knot before he could complete it.'

Clara walked up the stairs behind him, incredulous that anyone could board up a house like this for thirty years. Layers of dust were on the family portraits which lined the uncarpeted stairs.

'Yes, thirty years since anyone lived here,' Gareth mused as they went down a cavernous corridor, footsteps echoing on the scrappy wooden floorboards. There were signs of work in progress, too—a box filled with rolls of wallpaper, paste pots and paint pots and the scent of fresh varnish. 'Grandpa just shut the whole place up long before I was born. Nobody's lived here since. Nobody's even visited the place.'

'Do you know why?'

'I've asked a million times. But Grandpa just looks sad and refuses to talk about it. The funny thing is, no one else will discuss it either.'

'What do you mean—no one else?'

'No one in the family. None of the villagers. They all get that same sad look in their eyes, though, so I'm sure they know what the story is.' He laughed again. 'Quite an intriguing little mystery, really. The abandoned Manor of Rhossana Bay.'

Clara knew it had something to do with Jared. She longed to find out more but clearly would have to wait for Jared himself to tell her. He'd never forgive her if she tried to pry behind his back and she wouldn't blame him. So instead she asked, 'Did you and Susie know it would be like this when you moved in?'

'Oh, yes. Grandpa explained it all to us at the reception. He said he wanted the Manor to be completely redeemed—whatever that means. He said we could make any changes we liked and he'd foot the bill. He had some theory about a young pair of newlyweds in love. Said it would fill the house with laughter and sunlight—dispel the dark memories.'

Clara shivered. Jared had so many of his own...

'This is your room, Clara.' Pushing open a door, he motioned her inside. 'The housekeeper tells me there are fresh towels in the bathroom and a kettle with tea and coffee for you to use in the bedroom.'

'Thank you. It's lovely.' She smiled with relief at the brightly painted bedroom, brand-new silk wallpaper on the walls in a delicious shade of lemon. An inviting four-poster bed dominated the room, reminding her of home, only this one was white whereas Jared's bed was dark wood, and the fat lemon duvet looked like heaven to her tired eyes.

'When you wake up, just go down to the dining room. Fourth on the left downstairs along the main corridor. The housekeeper will have left a cooked breakfast on the hot plates. Just help yourself and feel free to ring the hospital, too.'

As soon as she was alone she stopped smiling and stared around her. She asked herself what on earth was going on there. No wonder Jared had gone slowly berserk the closer this marriage came. The Manor was in a terrible state of disrepair, and to discover it had been boarded up for nearly thirty years was just incredible. But why thirty years? Jared had left Rhossana when he was seventeen. That put the date of his departure twenty years ago. Not thirty.

Exhaustion hit her in sudden waves and she realised she was too tired even to think. Closing the thick lemon silk curtains, she undressed and slid into bed. She was asleep as soon as her head hit the pillow.

When she woke she took a bath in silent luxury and told herself she must not even consider indulging in a cooked breakfast. She was so hungry. And the weather had changed while she slept. Wind whistled round the house now, rattling the doors and windows as it blew in from the sea.

She arrived downstairs in a pale blue woollen dress to find Harrison was already eating in the dining room. Silver trays of eggs, kidneys, mushrooms, sausages and fried bread sat on the mahogany table. Clara's mouth watered. She kept Rachel firmly in her mind and refused to be tempted.

'Where is everyone?'

'Mr Gareth's been at the hospital for three hours,'

Harrison told her. 'There's no change in Miss Susie's condition, though. She's stable but still unconscious.'

Clara sighed. 'I'd better ring London, see if there's any news from Mr Blackheath.'

She was just about to go back to the hall to use the phone when she heard the chopper. Heart pounding, she raced to the French windows. The jet-black helicopter was unmistakable against stark grey skies. 'BLACKHEATH' was written along the tail in gold letters, the company logo emblazoned in red beside it.

'Jared!' she called excitedly, and flung open the doors, rushing out into the half-mown gardens as the chopper hovered, looking for a place to land. Waist-high grass spun in dizzy circles, flattening as the helicopter moved in to land. It shifted closer to the house on a flat piece of newly mown grass.

The black door flashed open. Jared stepped out, every inch the multi-millionaire tycoon in a black three-piece suit. The wind ruffled his hair. It tossed the black jacket back from his powerful chest. He ran towards Clara, head bent as the helicopter took off again and flew away. They collided in each other's arms.

'I came as soon as I heard,' he said against her cheek. 'How is she?'

'Just terrible.' Clara's voice cracked as she drew back to look at him, hair blowing like a blonde storm around her lovely face. 'I burst into tears as soon as I saw her. Bandages everywhere, wires attached to her...and she just lies there. Doesn't move, doesn't speak...'

'I rang the hospital on my way here. They said she was stable. I guess that could mean just about anything.'

'They didn't tell me you rang, and I asked more than once.'

'You had enough on your plate,' he said deeply. 'I didn't want to worry you. I also didn't want to tear you from Susie's bedside just to talk to me on the phone.'

'But I was frantic with worry!'

'Well, never mind. I'm here now. And I'll do everything I can to help. I'll take you to and from the hospital, sit and talk to Susie with you—in fact, I won't leave Wales until Susie's woken up again.'

Groaning with relief, she laid her head on his strong shoulder. His hand caressed her tousled hair and she felt safe, so safe after the chaos of the last twenty-four hours. Jared smelled of fresh sea air, of after-shave and clean skin. The sea breeze blew strongly across them as the storm built.

'What made you stay here?' Jared asked above her head, and his voice was edged with darkness.

Tensing, she said, 'Honestly darling—I tried every hotel in the district but they were all full. It's the holiday season.'

'So it is…'

Gulls flew inland to escape the storm. Spray from the black rocks flew high as the sea rushed in faster. Clouds darkened ominously overhead and as she looked up into Jared's face she saw that darkness echoed in his eyes.

'The Manor.' He stared over her head. 'I haven't seen it in over twenty years.'

Clara watched him but he did not watch her. He watched the house. Its crumbling walls and windows seemed to watch him too, as though they had been waiting for him to arrive home.

'It's in a terrible state,' Clara said, to dispel the atmosphere.

'Oh, yes. Locked up. Shut down.' His voice deepened. 'And frozen in time like us—like all of us. Everything stopped that day. Everything…'

She stroked his cold cheek, trying to get him to look at her, not his nemesis. 'What day, darling? When did everything stop?'

He continued to watch the house. 'Which room did you sleep in? Does it face the sea?'

'Yes. It faces the sea that way.' She pointed across the lawns to the grey wrath of the water. 'It has a four-poster bed and a balcony.'

His hands tightened on her body. 'Is it a blue room? With a painting of a woman on the wall? Just above the fireplace…a dark-haired woman in sapphires?'

Shivering again, she said, 'No, it's lemon-yellow. And there are no paintings in it.' The description of the woman sounded like his mother. She would have been younger then. Had Owain had a portrait done during their affair or afterwards? It was difficult to work out the time scale because Jared simply wouldn't answer straight questions and she didn't know what happened after the affair ended.

'At least he had some shred of decency, then,' Jared said under his breath, startling her. 'I'd begun to doubt that when I heard you were staying here. I thought maybe he'd put you straight into the room, that blue bedroom with the portrait...' His voice faded into the storm.

Clara asked softly, 'Is that the room where your mother—?'

'Have you been in any other rooms?'

She stared for a second, then said patiently, 'No, just the dining room. Oh—and the hall.'

He went very pale. He gazed at the house in silence. What was he thinking? Her arms held him tighter, as though trying to blend with him and reach his secret heart. The wind battered at them as he bent his head to kiss her cheek.

'All right, darling?' she whispered.

'I can't believe I'm actually here,' he said thickly. 'With the scent of Rhossana all around me and the sea breeze in my hair.'

'How does it feel?'

'I don't want to stay here. I'll move us both out now. Today.' He looked away from her, back at the house. 'Don't tell me the hotels are booked. I'll get them unbooked, no matter what I have to offer. You know as well as I do that money—enough money—can buy anything. Where's Harrison?'

'In the dining room eating his breakfast.'

'The dining room?' He relaxed fractionally. 'That's at the back, isn't it? And there are French windows. I remember. We can easily walk round and get in that way, can't we?'

Without another word he took her hand and strode across the lawns towards the rear of the Manor. Clara

could not shake the feeling that it watched him as
closely as he watched it. Like an old friend welcoming him home after a terrible argument, it seemed to
have such strong living presence that she saw it as
battered, broken and in need of help. Like someone
in a time-warp and just waiting for the one person
who can help them out of it. And she was so certain
that Jared was the one this house needed. She could
almost hear it whispering his name with pleasure as
the storm rushed around the eaves, the pillars, the long
wide windows.

Jared seemed aware of it too as he walked towards
it. Only he did not feel pleased to see his old friend
again. Every line of his face was tense with hostile
rejection as he made his way across the lawns to the
back of the house.

'Mr Blackheath!' Harrison's voice called suddenly.

They both stopped, looked towards the front door
and saw Harrison standing there. He waved cheerfully
in his chauffeur's uniform. Jared's fingers tightened
in Clara's.

'Damn it.' He went even paler than before as he
was forced to change direction and walk towards the
front door.

He stumbled.

'Darling—!' Clara stared up in concern.

'The grass was damp, don't make a fuss!' he bit
out thickly, but his skin reddened and he avoided her
eyes before carrying on determinedly until they
reached the white steps at the front of the house.

He stopped dead at the steps. He stood facing the
sea as though refusing point-blank to even glance in-

1st

FIRST PAST THE POST

Scratch & Win...
up to **4 FREE BOOKS**
and a **MYSTERY GIFT**

See inside ↗

Race to the finish and get up to
FIVE FREE GIFTS!

NO RISK, NO OBLIGATION TO BUY... NOW OR EVER!

HERE'S HOW TO PLAY:

1. Flip that lucky coin in the air and scratch off the silver boxes. Now, depending on where you placed in the race, you will receive up to four specially selected Mills & Boon® novels from the Presents™ series, and an exciting Mystery Gift - FREE!

2. Simply return this card and you will receive up to four Presents novels, which are yours to keep, absolutely free.

Why Would We Offer Such A Deal?

The editors at Mills & Boon simply want you to enjoy what thousands are already enjoying: the convenience of home delivery of the latest Presents novels. Imagine receiving the best romance novels at your door at least a month before they are available in the shops. And better yet, postage and packing is entirely at our expense.

FREE Books
A FREE Gift
and more...

Scratch here to be eligible to receive a Mystery Gift.

Scratch off the silver box to see if you were 'First Past the Post'

SEE CLAIM CHART BELOW

YES! I have scratched the silver boxes above. Please rush me all the free gifts for which I qualify, as shown on the claim chart below. I understand that I am under no obligation to purchase any books, as explained overleaf. I am over 18 years of age.

P8DI

MS/MRS/MISS/MR   INITIALS

SURNAME   BLOCK CAPITALS PLEASE

ADDRESS

POSTCODE

CLAIM CHART

For third place you get **2 free books & a Mystery Gift!** **3rd**

For second place you get **3 free books & a Mystery Gift!** **2nd**

For first place you get **4 free books & a Mystery Gift!** **1st**

THE READER SERVICE : HERE'S HOW IT WORKS

Accepting the free books and gift places you under no obligation to buy anything. You may keep the books and gift and return the despatch note marked "cancel". If we do not hear from you, about a month later we will send you 6 brand new books and invoice you just £2.30* each. That's the complete price - there is no extra charge for postage and packing. You may cancel at any time, otherwise every month we'll send you 6 more books, which you may either purchase or return - the choice is yours.

*Prices subject to change without notice.

THE READER SERVICE™
FREEPOST SEA3794
CROYDON
Surrey
CR9 3AQ

▼ DETACH AND RETURN THIS CARD TODAY. NO STAMP NEEDED! ▼

side the open doorway and Clara suddenly realised why.

It's the hall, she thought. He's avoiding the hall. But why? Staring in, she saw the chandelier wink at her as it moved in the wind, yellowing crystal tinkling.

'Yes, sir?' Harrison asked.

'Get Miss Maye's case from upstairs,' Jared said without looking at him. 'She's leaving. So are you. I'll get us all booked into a hotel before nightfall.'

'My case is packed and ready.' Clara tried to be helpful to speed up the process for them all. 'I left it on the floor next to the bed.'

'Right you are, miss.' Harrison looked perplexed but didn't argue, simply turned and went up the shabby staircase.

Jared remained where he was, monolithic, expressionless and staring at the grey seas. He was too distressed, clearly, to answer any more searching questions. And she didn't want to upset him even more, certainly not until they were alone. She would ask him later, if at all. Meanwhile, she gave him her silent support, holding his arm and cuddling up to him with her blonde head on his dark shoulder. She too gazed out to sea and wondered what traumas this house had witnessed in its mysterious past.

'Sorry I was so long, sir.' Harrison came clattering down the stairs with the cases. 'Had to get my case, too. Hadn't even packed it. Then I forgot my shaving kit and had to go back. Mrs H always says I'd forget my own head if it wasn't screwed on.'

'For once I agree with her,' Jared drawled with an

attempt at humour. He turned his back on the mournful house and the whispering hall. 'Come on. Let's get going.'

They walked to the limousine.

But at that moment another car came into sight. Clara looked up with a sinking heart to see Owain Llewellyn's grey Bentley gliding towards them down that long tree-lined drive.

'It's him,' Jared said under his breath, and stopped to stare at the car as it flashed into the cold grey light. 'He must have heard the helicopter.'

She frowned. 'But he was at the hospital, Jared. He wouldn't have heard—'

'This town is smaller than it looks, Clara.' He gave a wintry smile. 'How many helicopters do you think touch down on the lawns of the Manor every day?'

Reaching a standstill, the Bentley seemed ominous as the grey rear door clicked open. Owain Llewellyn stepped out. His pale eyes fixed on Jared in the same way Jared's had fixed on the house. Clara wondered for the first time precisely how Owain felt about the affair which had wrecked Jared's family when he was still a boy. It would have been easier to guess if she'd had more information.

Still impeccably dressed in black, Owain walked towards Jared. His silver hair blew around his once handsome face. The Manor seemed to hold its breath.

'Mr Blackheath. What a pleasant surprise.'

'A surprise? I doubt it. You either heard my helicopter or saw it.'

'My chauffeur saw it. So did the nurses. I was told, yes. I came here at once.'

'Wanted to see me standing here, did you?'

Winds battered at the trees on the estate and gulls cried overhead as Owain Llewellyn faced the powerful man that little eight-year-old Jared Blackheath had become.

'It's a sight I've wanted to see for years,' Owain said. 'And it gives me hope. All this could have been cleared up so long ago. You're not the only one who suffered, Mr Blackheath. Not the only one who still suffers.'

Jared's face was implacable. 'I don't doubt that you've suffered. But I don't intend to take responsibility for it. I was eight years old. How old were you?'

'You're never too old to fall in love,' he whispered. 'Your mother did everything she could to stop herself loving me. And I tried to help her. I swear I didn't touch her for the first two years. We both resisted, but in the end love was more powerful than either of us. We couldn't help ourselves. We were swept away by the sheer force of the thing. Try to remember the temptations, Jared. Seeing each other for those two years, not being able to have each other, be with each other. When we finally gave in, the passion just drowned us both. We couldn't think of anything but each other. We were selfish, I know, but it *was* love.'

'Is that why you married another woman a year after your affair with my mother ended?'

Clara listened as impassively as she could. Carefully keeping her face free from expression, she took in every word without reacting to it. She knew she must stand by Jared, no matter how many skeletons came dancing out of the cupboards.

'I remarried because your mother wouldn't see me. She wouldn't even speak to me. She was crucified by guilt. So was I. And waking up every morning in this damned house was more than I could bear.'

'At least,' said Jared, 'you have the decency to admit that!'

'I was haunted by what I'd done to you.'

Jared looked quickly away. That seemed more intolerable to him than anything else Owain had yet said.

'But now—don't you see?' Owain stepped towards him. 'It's all come full circle. My grandson fell in love with the one woman who can bring us all together. We can heal the past now. All of us.'

Jared's smile was cynical. 'Is that why you gave them this house as a wedding present? To force me back down here, regardless of how long it took?'

Owain hesitated. 'Yes...'

'A wedding present? Do you really find that appropriate?'

'They're in love,' Owain defended himself, but his skin reddened. 'I know it must seem thoughtless, but only in the short term. They know nothing of what happened. They can only do good. They'll bring hope and laughter back into the house.'

'While my father—!' Jared bit out hoarsely, then broke off.

The wind blew harsh and cold. The first faint specks of rain began to fall, just odd little dashes on the face, the hands, but enough to make them all look up to the overcast sky.

'I'm ending this conversation,' Jared said. 'It's

gone far enough. Harrison—get in the car and start it. We're leaving.'

'Yes, sir!' Harrison was round-eyed with fascination as he leapt to the driver's door.

'Mr Llewellyn.' Jared arched cold brows at him. 'I don't wish to be rude, but I would prefer not to meet you again while I'm in Wales. Please time your visits to the hospital so they don't coincide with mine. I suggest you discuss it with Gareth. And by the way—I also have no intention of ever visiting the Manor again. Ever.' With a curt nod, he strode to the limousine.

Sliding into the grey leather seats, Clara was utterly silent. Her face was as expressionless, as it had been through the exchange, but her mind was racing.

'Please…' Owain followed them. 'You can't let it end like this.'

'It ended thirty years ago.' Jared got into the car, shut the door with a sharp thud and leaned forward to tell Harrison, 'Take us to the hospital. Immediately.'

'Yes, sir.'

'And Harrison,' he said as they pulled away, 'if you remember one word of that conversation—you're fired.'

'Forgotten it already, sir.'

Jared leaned back against the seats tensely. They drove down the tree-lined drive as rain began to fall. The windscreen wipers were switched on smoothly. If Owain Llewellyn watched them go, Clara did not know it; she was too busy concentrating on Jared's feelings.

Silently, she slipped her hand in his.

His fingers linked with hers, squeezed them tight. 'Thank you. It must have been difficult to just stand there and say nothing.'

'Not that difficult. I love you.'

He exhaled harshly and pulled her into his arms. The warmth of his body was at odds with the icy cold of his tough face and fingers. Clara buried her face in his neck, kissing him.

'He's such a very old man now,' Jared murmured. 'It was a shock to see him again at the wedding. But to see him on the steps of the Manor…'

'If only I knew what else had happened there, darling,' she ventured softly against the black material of his jacket, not risking eye contact in case he withdrew because of it. 'If you ever want to tell me—'

'No.'

She lifted her head, then, to look into his eyes, disappointed. He shot Harrison a brief glance and she realised as he looked back at her that his raised-brow expression meant he wouldn't talk here.

Of course, she thought. Harrison had already seen and heard too much. Jared was a deeply private person, for all his fame. He lived behind a series of force fields, each one impenetrable and closely guarded. One by one, as his trust for Clara had grown, he had lifted each force field for her to step inside. He certainly had no intention of ever letting anyone else as close to him as she was.

Even though the screen could have protected him from being overheard, Harrison would know by the mere presence of that screen that Jared was deeply upset and talking about something very personal connected to the Manor and Llewellyn. This was a man who understood the minutiae of personal relationships. An odd quirk for someone so complex, so good at guarding his deepest secret. Only Clara was close enough to guess at it.

But how close am I? she wondered as they drove on. What really happened in that house to those people?

Soon they reached the hospital. Jared came in with her. He went white when he saw Susie. For thirty seconds he stood at her bedside, staring down in silence. Clara understood. It was a shock to see all those tubes and wires and bandages.

'There aren't many things money can't buy,' he said with husky regret. 'But life is one of them.' His hand took Susie's. 'She's such a lovely girl. I can't bear to see her like this. Why do these things always happen to the people one truly loves?'

Clara moved to stand beside him, kissed his handsome cheek. 'It's so wonderful to have you here, darling. I can't tell you how much it means to me. How many other men would stop their whole world in order to come and help me save my best friend?'

'Anyone with any decency,' he said gently, and kissed her.

CHAPTER SIX

JARED found rooms for them at The Grange. A big country house converted into a hotel, it stood on the outskirts of the town in private grounds. He got a suite for himself and Clara and a double room for Harrison. It cost him a very large sum of money. He apparently gave the previous occupants enough for a five-star luxury cruise in the Caribbean, but it was worth it to ensure he and Clara didn't have to spend a night at the Manor.

It was dark as they drove to the hotel. Ten-thirty and they were both very tired. Although the rain had started late afternoon, it had come in intermittent showers. Now the storm was about to break. Distant thunder rippled ever closer. Heavy rain cascaded down, hurtling against the windows of the limousine like gunfire. The windscreen wipers worked overtime. Lightning flared in the troubled night sky.

Jared held Clara in his arms in companionable silence. It was cosy in the rear seats. She felt like a little girl again, before the tragedy of the fire had taken her parents from her... She thought of security and the shattering of it. They had that in common, she and Jared. Both had lost a safe haven at the tender age of eight and been forced to carve their own niche in a crazy world. But how had Jared lost his security? She still didn't know the truth. All she knew was that it had something to do with that manor house. His true feelings towards it had been blindingly clear as he stood in front of it today. He was both frightened and angered by the sight of it. Most notably by the hallway. It was as though the very threshold of the house haunted him. Why?

Clara believed in fate. With every moment they spent here in Rhossana her belief grew stronger. It comforted her to think that way. If Susie's accident had been an act of fate to bring Jared here, that meant that Susie would recover. It was only fate that she'd had the accident. That was all she could bear to believe, because if it wasn't fate…

Shifting uneasily, Clara tried not to imagine the worst.

'Darling?' Jared murmured.

'Just thinking about Susie.' Her voice was husky. 'I try not to even consider the possibility that she might die.'

'Susie's always been a fighter. She'll pull through.'

'Do you really think so?'

'Life is too precious to her. She won't just slip away into the dark without a struggle.'

Relief swamped her. 'I'm so pleased you're here, Jared. I don't know how I'd cope with this if you weren't.'

'You know I'd never desert you. Or Susie.'

Tears blinded her briefly. Blinking them back, afraid to appear too emotional even though the strain on her over the last twenty-four hours had been enormous, Clara kissed him.

'We're too closely connected,' Jared said against

her lips. 'All three of us. I know I'm not an orphan but I've always felt like one, and that makes the difference.'

'I guess it does.'

'When I first met you, every time I looked at you I thought: She has no one but me to protect her.'

Clara smiled, stroked his cheek with one hand. 'Darling…'

'I still think it from time to time. Not as much as when we first met. But often enough to remember I'm the only protection you've got.'

'I think it's strange that you identify with orphans when you are not, in fact, an orphan. Why is that, Jared? Is it something to do with your father's death?'

His dark lashes flickered. He bent his head to kiss her. She knew she was being silenced again, and although she noted with interest the point at which he terminated the conversation, she nevertheless did not fight. He'd been through enough for one day. They both had. Her arms wrapped around his neck as she closed her eyes and surrendered to his loving mouth.

But as passion began to flare between them, Harrison said, 'Here we are, sir. The Grange.'

The car slid in through the gates of the hotel as they sat up. Rain was sluicing down the windows. It distorted the view of the ivy-covered redbrick hotel, but in the carriage light above the double doors the elegant dark green sign announced its name in yellow letters.

Jared and Clara raced up the steps. For a second they stood in the bright-lit foyer, shaking themselves free of rainwater. Then Jared strode to the reception desk, picked up the keys and led Clara to the lifts.

Harrison went off to his own room.

Their suite was beautiful. Large, imposing and luxuriously furnished, it nonetheless had a homely feel to it, as though they actually lived there. A cosy fireplace was surrounded by plush couches and armchairs; there were long curtains at the windows and flowers blooming in antique vases. The rain pitter-pattering against the windows made its warmth even more welcoming.

'I've booked it indefinitely.' Jared shouldered out of the black jacket and slung it over an armchair. 'Who knows how long we'll be here?'

'That's a point.' Clara looked around for a phone. 'I'd better ring Mitch, give him this number. If that role comes through I need to know immediately.'

'What will you do if they need you in London before Susie's better?'

'I...' The thought of losing that role was unbearable. She'd waited all her life for it. But great roles were not as valuable as great friends. 'I guess I'll just have to cross that bridge when I come to it. I can't abandon Susie.'

'It's a terrible choice to have to make.'

'Sophie's choice.' Picking up the phone, she resolutely punched out Mitch's London home number.

'Hello?' Mitch answered on the fourth ring. In the background a girl was laughing, and Mitch's voice had a sexy edge to it.

'Aha!' Clara laughed. 'Caught you red-handed!'

His voice grew panic-stricken. 'Is everything all right? You haven't got bad news? Susie's not—?'

'She's still alive, Mitch, don't worry.'

'What are her chances? Realistically?'

'The doctors say fifty-fifty. But I say better than average, and I'll be staying here until she pulls through.'

'Wales, then.' His voice crackled with interference from the storm. 'At long last.'

'At long last, yes.' She smiled wryly.

'What's it like?'

'Very pretty, from what I've seen of it so far.'

'Wasn't he born there? In Rhossana—'

'Rhossana Bay, yes. He was born here,' Clara interrupted him, aware of Jared listening. 'But, as I say, I might be here for some time. So let me give you the telephone number of the hotel.'

Mitch took it down as she recited it. He promised to call as soon as he had news on Rachel, then Clara bade him farewell and replaced the receiver. Turning, she found Jared watching her with narrowed eyes.

'Cosy chat?' His voice was hostile.

Taken aback by his tone, she answered cautiously, 'He was very friendly and concerned, yes.'

'And just when did you tell him that I'd never taken you to Wales before?' he bit out under his breath. 'Just when did you tell him I was born here and had never been back?'

'Darling...' She was dry-mouthed as she realised he thought she'd betrayed him to Mitch. 'I haven't told him anything at all about—'

'What else does he know, Clara?'

'Just that Susie—'

'About me! About me, Clara! Not about Susie or you or your career, but about me and my background in Wales!'

'Jared, I swear to you he knows nothing about—'

'I just stood here and listened to your conversation! You didn't have to explain a thing, did you? He asked the questions and you gave the replies. Only an idiot would assume you hadn't discussed me, my personal history, my background, my aversion to Wales—' He broke off, breathing hoarsely, then shouted, 'What else have you discussed with him, Clara? Tell me!'

In the stunned silence that followed, she struggled to accept that he seriously believed she'd betrayed him throughout their relationship. It was incredible. Did he really think her capable of such treachery?

'He's always been closer to you than any other man but me!' Jared was beginning to sound jealous. 'I should have known you'd tell him everything I told you! From the minute I met you, he was the one you turned to, confided in, trusted—'

'I turned to Susie! Not Mitch!'

'And have you told Susie anything? Of course you have! Why do I even bother to ask, you indiscreet, disloyal little—?'

'Jared, for heaven's sake calm down!' she shouted back at him. She was losing her own temper after the strain of the day, and was too tired to figure out why they were really shouting at each other; she was feeling too stressed and emotionally exhausted. 'I haven't told anyone anything! Not a thing!'

'That's what I always believed. Until now. That

phone call horrified me, Clara. Mitch shouldn't know those things. He shouldn't even know I don't like Wales. *No one* should know that.'

'He didn't mention anything about you not liking Wales, Jared. And the reason is because he doesn't know. Nor do I, for that matter. This is the first time you've ever actually admitted it straight out!'

'Oh, but you guessed it way back, didn't you?'

'Only because you kept avoiding the place and refusing to talk about it!'

'And you know why?'

'No, I don't know why, Jared! You've only told me half the story and whenever I ask for more you either silence me or hand me rambling explanations!'

'Rambling explanations?' He strode to her, bristling from head to foot with rage. 'What the hell do you mean by that? I've got every right to keep my own counsel on any subject I like! Just because you're my girlfriend doesn't mean you own me! Or that you have a right to demand I tell you a damned thing!'

Tears pricked her eyes. 'Oh, thanks!'

'Look—I've always steered clear of Wales. So what? I'm a busy man! I fly around the world and back before most people have had their breakfast! If I haven't visited Wales for twenty years that's my business and my decision! And I don't have to explain that decision to anyone. To *anyone*, do you hear?' he shouted, towering over her in a way that left her breathless as she stared up at his furious face. 'Least of all that intrusive agent of yours!'

Fiercely, she shot back, 'He is not intrusive and I have never told him anything personal!'

'You spend far too much time with him,' he accused jealously. 'You're always with him when I'm away.'

'Oh, what rubbish!' She was dimly aware that she was bickering with him as though they were an old married couple. 'I'm usually alone, reading scripts.'

'You saw him this time while I was away!'

'Because I had a test! What's the matter with you? Mitch is my agent. Even when I am with him, we're talking business. Film, television—industry. He's not interested in my private life any more than I'm interested in his.'

'Has he ever made a pass at you?' he demanded thickly.

'What...?' she gasped in disbelief.

'Answer the question!' He gripped her slim shoulders with a sudden anger that shocked her. 'Has Mitch ever made a pass at you!'

Stunned, she couldn't speak for several seconds. It wasn't merely that he had asked the question, nor even that they had discussed it fully when they first met. No, what shocked her most was that he quite obviously believed it. She could see it in his eyes, hear it in the tone of his voice. When Jared was hurt or jealous or scared he always showed it as anger. It seemed to be a common flaw in men, or perhaps it was more of a self-defence mechanism. How they needed to hide their feelings! Particularly those that made them vulnerable. Probably the only feeling men felt able to show directly was anger. It hid a multitude of sins and did not lay them open to attack.

'Answer me, damn you!' He was really angry now.

'If you don't I'll be forced to believe that Mitch
has—'

'He's never made a pass at me.'

'Then why did you hesitate just now?'

'Because I couldn't believe you'd think it, let alone
ask it!'

'And if he did make a pass at you,' he demanded
thickly, 'would you accept it?'

'How can you even ask me that?' she exploded.
'You should know me better than this! I'm a one-man
woman; I always have been. I don't play around, I'm
not promiscuous and I wouldn't dream of betraying
the man I loved—even with a kiss, let alone anything
more serious.'

Thunder crashed outside the darkened windows. It
was closer now, almost overhead, and the lightning
which flared seconds later illuminated the harsh
planes of his troubled face. His eyes were black. Yet
there was a suspicion and mistrust in their depths
which she had never seen before. It went beyond mere
jealousy and into the realms of unreasoning fear.

Suddenly she knew what was wrong. It struck her
so forcibly that it hurt her, made her catch her breath.
His anger had fooled her. Her exhaustion had been
too great for her to read the emotional clues he was
sending her. It just showed her how completely she
needed to be on her toes while they were here, and
never stop reading his feelings, no matter how tired
she was herself.

'But how stupid of me.' Her voice was a pained
whisper. 'This isn't about Mitch at all, is it? It's
about Wales.'

He stared at her in silence.

'It's because you're here, on Welsh soil, and today you spoke with Owain Llewellyn on the steps of the Manor, where it all happened thirty years ago.'

'No,' he bit out thickly, but his hands tightened on her shoulders. 'It's got nothing to do with that.'

'What happened thirty years ago, Jared?'

'It's Mitch,' he insisted furiously, avoiding her eyes while his hands hurt her shoulders. 'I don't like you spending so much time with him. I don't want him around. I want him out of the picture. I want him out of your life for good.'

'Jared...!'

'I don't know what I'm saying!' he muttered hoarsely. 'I can't think properly. I just sense danger, Clara.'

With that, he broke away from her. There was a brief silence. He was breathing hard and she saw him make a concerted effort to regain his self-assurance. His hands were on his hips. He was trying to regain his composure, and, though she knew the struggle was tough because of the emotional pressure he was under, she also knew she must not interfere or make him feel in any way weakened.

'I'm sorry.' He turned to look at her, calmer now but still very much on edge. 'When you were on the phone to Mitch I suddenly thought, Wait a second. He's been close to her for eight years. He sees her when I'm away. He knows a lot about her and now he must know a lot about me, too. Not only that, but he's a publicity man, and his access to the media is dangerous.'

She blinked, studying him in silence because she couldn't argue with that. It was true. Mitch had friends in every area of the media and he was a talkative, friendly man. He *could* let slip some piece of information that would be better kept to himself.

'I won't have him in your life at this point,' Jared said. 'Not while we're here in Wales. Anything you say to him could be misinterpreted, twisted round or—worse—interpreted correctly. That would be disastrous. I do not want *anything* about me or Wales or the Manor getting into the press. I couldn't tolerate it. So Mitch has to go.' He paused before dropping the bombshell. 'Maybe even permanently.'

Clara struggled for calm but was breathless, appalled.

He doesn't mean what he's saying about Mitch, she told herself. He can't possibly. Jared had stood by her in her career from the moment they'd met and was very proud of her. Why would he turn against her and damage it now? Because I don't know what actually happened here, she realised with a shock.

In her mind's eye she saw the Manor, but then she focused for some reason on the great hall, the cobwebs around that crystal chandelier and the whispers of time as the house seemed to reach out to Jared. She didn't know what it meant. But he did. He knew precisely what was going on. And he had the right to preserve that secret from her—from the world, too, even if it meant temporarily putting Mitch on hold.

Reminding herself that a good general always knows when to retreat, Clara said, 'Okay, darling. I won't talk to Mitch again while we're in Wales.'

'That may not be enough,' he said tightly. 'I may want him out of the picture for good.'

Breathless, she said as calmly as possible, 'I can't risk that until I know one way or the other about Rachel.'

'You'll get the part of Rachel regardless of who your agent is.'

'But they know where to contact me while I'm with Mitch. I've been with him for eight years. We're too well known as actress and agent.'

'If they want you, they'll contact you through me, not him.'

Moistening dry lips, she was able to stay calm only because she was so sure he'd feel differently once they were out of Wales. 'All right, darling. I'll certainly think seriously about it.'

'I don't want you on the phone to him again while we're here.'

'I just agreed to that, Jared. You can take all my calls.'

His mouth tightened. 'And don't sound so damned patient, either! I'm not mad! I don't need to be humoured! Do at least *try* to see it from my point of view.'

'But you won't tell me your point of view, Jared.'

He looked away, then bit out thickly, 'All right. I'm in Wales for the first time in twenty years and the skeletons are just about to start trooping out of the cupboards accompanied by a brass band. Look at what Harrison overheard today. Look at what Mitch already knows.'

'He knows almost nothing.'

'But he figured that "nothing" out for himself, didn't he? This is how secrets leak out, Clara. Piece by tiny piece. It's never all at once. It's like a jigsaw puzzle. People put it together slowly. At first it looks like irrelevant information. But after a couple more pieces it becomes an enticing mystery. People always want to solve mysteries whenever they find them. Now, I believe you haven't said anything that you consider a breach of confidence to Mitch. But he's nonetheless got the first few small pieces of my private jigsaw puzzle.'

'I haven't given them to him.'

'The mysterious jigsaw puzzle called Jared Blackheath that the world has never been able to solve.' His voice deepened. 'And I don't want to be solved, Clara. Not by anyone outside this room.'

'I...' She felt the leap of love in her heart, realising what he was telling her and feeling as though she'd just got through the final barrier and was about to pass the final test.

'That's right,' he said huskily as he watched the truth dawn on her beautiful face and fill her with love. 'I trust you. But I don't trust anybody else. Not my mother, not Harrison, not Mitch, not the men I work with, do business with—nobody. Only you.'

'Darling...'

'And that's why it's imperative that while we're here you have no further contact with the outside world. Just one unguarded word and Mitch could get another glimpse of the full picture. Then it's a hop away from his unguarded word to a reporter.'

'I can't believe you'd think Mitch would be so

stupid,' she said under her breath. 'Or that I would, either. I realise Mitch has already guessed that you hate Wales, but if—'

'It only takes one word, Clara, to make the penny drop.'

'But that unguarded word won't come,' she pointed out, 'if you tell me precisely which pieces of information might be dangerous.'

He gave a tight smile, his voice roughening. 'You're asking me to tell you everything. But I can't. Not right now. Maybe never. Who knows?'

'But if you don't tell me, I might unguardedly—'

'Quite.' He shot her a brooding look. 'And Mitch already knows too much. He'll be sitting in London right now, wondering. Mysteries are like that. They fix in the brain. They revolve and revolve and they don't stop revolving until they fall into place. He'll wait to solve it. Even if it takes twenty years.'

She felt the pain show in her eyes because she knew what he said was true.

'I don't blame Mitch for this, you understand,' Jared said deeply. 'I just have the intelligence to recognise human nature for what it is and deal with it accordingly.'

Clara drew an unsteady breath. 'But if I fire Mitch for no good reason he'll be within his rights to feel betrayed. And you know how people can react when they feel betrayed.'

'I know exactly how people react when they feel betrayed!' His eyes blackened with memories. 'I've lived with it since I was eight years old.'

'Darling,' she said huskily, 'what happened here?'

He closed his eyes and said nothing.

'If only you'd tell me,' she whispered. For a second she was silent, watching him. Then she moved to him, slid her arms lovingly around his neck. 'I could help. If I knew what it was, I could help you with it, make sure nobody else found out, keep it—'

'No!' he muttered hoarsely, but his hands slid to her waist and he held her close to him. 'I've never told anyone. Never talked. Not since I left here. Before that, even. Not since—' He broke off. His heart thudded hard against his chest. 'It's late. I'm tired. I want to go to bed. We can talk another time. Right now, I need love—as much as you can give me. All night. Clara…darling…' He pulled her against his powerful body with a hunger that made her breathless, but before she could speak his head swooped, that hot mouth closed urgently over hers and the sheer force of his angry passion brought a wild response from her.

She was reeling under the full onslaught of his kiss. This had come right out of the blue. She loved it when it was like this. A sudden roar of desire like the opening of a furnace. A girl could get burnt to death very pleasurably in the blast. Even now his hard hands were getting harder—so was the rest of his body. It was so hot and so unexpected that it knocked her off her feet.

'I need you!' he bit out thickly against her mouth.

She didn't get a chance to reply. He picked her up, carried her across the living room and kicked open the bedroom door, not stopping except to kick it shut again before striding to the bed in darkness and putting her on it.

'I need this!' His eyes blazed like hot coals as he fell on her with an urgency that made her dizzy.

His hands were moving up her thighs before she could gasp in excited response. He spread them with those hard hands, very hard indeed as they stroked the soft flesh above her stockings. She could feel the rough hairs on the back of his hands. He was masterful, possessive, and he was busy removing her clothes as he kissed her mouth and whispered wicked things to her.

'Oh, Jared!' Her voice sounded as though it was melting with shocked pleasure, just as her body was, wet with excitement as his hand found her, stroked her without preamble before pulling her briefs down while she writhed in anticipation of those determined hands returning. Her moans filled the dark bedroom. His breathing was coarse and heavy. He knelt up suddenly to tear off his shirt and throw it to the floor, and the sight of his gorgeous chest made her moan even louder and whisper his name, encouraging him to carry on.

Her words inflamed him. Falling hungrily on her, he removed the last scraps of her clothing. Naked, she twisted wantonly against him, but he was in control, dominating instead of teasing her, stroking her soft nudity with firm expertise. Then his hands suddenly left her. He pushed his trousers off, his shorts, too, and Clara was more than ready when he moved to take her, pushing her thighs wide with his powerful knees.

'Lovely…' he growled with the first thrust, 'you're so lovely…'

It was fast and hot and quick.

Later, they lay exhausted in each other's arms. Her head was on his chest. His arm was around her. Love enveloped them in dreamy relaxation. She played with the hairs on his tanned skin and listened to the rain hurling itself against the windows and felt safe.

'I love you...'

He kissed the top of her head. 'I love you, too.' Then he laughed softly, his hand curling trustingly on her naked waist beneath the duvet. 'I wish I could think of a better way of saying that. Never can, though. Maybe one day I'll come up with the perfect phrase.'

'We could have that inscribed in Latin for our motto,' she said with a smile. '"Maybe one day." I wonder how you say "Maybe one day" in Latin?'

He went very still. And very silent. Unsmiling, he looked down into her eyes in the darkness.

'It's okay,' she whispered on his chest, looking up. 'I'll always love you. Secrets shared or no secrets shared.'

'Do you really mean that?'

'Of course. Love is love. There's no price tag on it. And no way out of it. It's like the elements, Jared. Uncontrollable and unstoppable.'

Tenderness lit his eyes. 'I wish we were at home. We could sneak downstairs and have a midnight snack!'

'Excellent plan!' she laughed. 'Why don't we see if they've got any room service? I'm famished!'

'I think it shuts at eleven or something equally inconvenient.' A smile touched his arrogant mouth. 'But

I could always make them an offer they couldn't refuse.'

'Well, if you do,' she said, coming to a snap decision, 'I fancy steak and chips!'

He stared. 'Chips?'

'Oh, pooh!' she groaned, burying her face in his warm hairy chest. 'I can't take the pressure any more! Give me food and lots of it!'

'Fried onions? Mushrooms?' He laughed as he reached for the phone. 'Extra chips and mayonnaise? How about a double chocolate milkshake?'

'And six double-decker club sandwiches!' she cried. 'Yippee!'

Jared punched out the number for room service and proceeded to play the charming and eccentric multimillionaire for all he was worth. Clara lay on his chest, smiling up at him with love and pride.

Everything would be all right.

So long as they could get from day to day without losing their sense of humour and their love for each other. So long as Susie pulled through. So long as Jared's secret did not blow up in their faces.

But would all of that really happen for them? Or was it asking too much of life? Everyone got hit by tragedy once in a while...

CHAPTER SEVEN

THE next three days were a strain on both of them. They spent most of their time at the hospital, coming back to the hotel to fall asleep in each other's arms.

In an effort to take as much pressure off both of them as possible, Jared told Reception to screen all calls. He gave them the names of his international aides, associates, personal assistants and major business colleagues. Only those calls were allowed to be put through to their suite. Everyone else had to leave a message.

'Including Mitch,' Jared had told her with a sharp lift to his brows.

The only bright light on the horizon was that Owain Llewellyn had treated Jared's wishes with respect.

'About time, too!' Jared had said tersely when he found out. 'My life is difficult enough without bumping into him at the hospital, too.'

But there was no danger of that. Owain had arranged to visit only during the night shift, which Gareth had insisted on taking. Clara and Jared took the day shift, but Gareth spent some time there during the day, too, unable to leave Susie when he was awake.

So they were at the hospital from nine in the morning until midnight, keeping a vigil on Susie—their lives seemed to revolve around her. She lay like

Sleeping Beauty, her face soft while her hair blazed Celtic red against the white pillows. Three times a day, a male physiotherapist came in and exercised her muscles for her—those that were not in plaster. While he worked on her, Clara and Jared went to the waiting room for a much-needed break of coffee and sandwiches.

Meanwhile, Jared's presence in Rhossana was causing excitable behaviour among the villagers. Almost every member of hospital staff appeared to have known him since he was born, and word had spread rapidly that he was in town. Not just in town, but sitting at the bedside of the tragic young Mrs Llewellyn with his famous girlfriend at his side. Staff from all over the hospital would walk slowly past the glass room in Intensive Care. They didn't disturb the quiet, disciplined atmosphere. They never spoke, never interfered, never entered the room. They just peered in at Jared with blatant fascination.

'Dai Williams,' Jared muttered as a man his own age in a doctor's white coat walked past and stared in. 'The vicar's son.'

And later his gaze lifted to a fresh-faced country girl in a nurse's uniform who gave Jared what Clara thought was a rather seductive smile as she walked past.

'Gwyneth Jones. She kissed me in the playground and told her friends she was going to marry me.'

Clara laughed. 'Well, at least she brings back good memories.'

'Kind of,' he drawled with a cynical smile. 'She changed her mind when I was eight and drew horrible pictures of my parents and Owain Llewellyn on the blackboard. But she was only a child, and you know how cruel children can be.'

'Your father too?' she asked with a frown, not quite understanding what the picture on the blackboard would have looked like. 'Why would she include him in the pictures?'

He hesitated and tensed, aware he had given something away. After a moment, he said evasively, 'Oh, I don't know. It was just a stupid picture.'

'I thought you said your father died when—'

'Forget it,' he clipped out curtly. 'I don't want to discuss it. Not now. Not in front of Susie.'

Late on Friday afternoon, the doctor stopped in on his rounds to see Susie and was pleased to note an improvement in her condition.

'We're getting far more signals from the brain than before,' he told Clara and Jared. 'No eye movement yet, and she's obviously still in the coma itself, but I anticipate a possible awakening within the next forty-eight hours.'

Clara and Jared were beside themselves with excitement. When Gareth arrived a few minutes later, the doctor was still there and told him the news too.

'You mean she could wake up any moment?' Gareth sank breathlessly down beside Susie and took her hand.

'I wouldn't go that far.' The doctor frowned. 'If this brain-wave response is what I think it is, I'd say it'll be another two days before we know for sure. Rapid eye movement is usually the last signal before they wake. According to Mr Blackheath and Miss

Maye, there's no evidence of that whatsoever. And they should know—they've been sitting here all day.'

'Yes...' Gareth turned to them. 'It's just after six. You've been here for ten hours. As there's been a marked improvement in her condition, why don't you both take a rest?'

'Oh, I don't want to leave her if she's likely to wake up any minute,' said Clara without hesitation.

'The doctor just told you she won't wake up for a couple of days yet, if then,' Gareth said. 'And you can leave her safely with me. I'll let you know if I see any sign of eye movement, or anything else to indicate she's coming round. I promise.'

With reluctance, Clara and Jared eventually agreed to leave Susie in Gareth's capable hands. Clara prayed Gareth would keep his word and let them know immediately there was a change.

Bright evening sunlight blazed down over the limousine as they drove out of the hospital car park. A handful of people stood by the grey slate gates, watching them as they had every night since they arrived.

'I wonder why nobody's told the press you're here?' Clara wondered aloud.

'Yes, I wondered that. You'd think someone would want to tell and sell. It is a good story, after all.' He frowned as they sped away down the main road, cross-town to the hotel. Shops were closed, car parks were deserted and only the lights in The King's Head showed signs of life. 'In fact, I've spent most of my adult life waiting for the story to appear. I wonder why it never has?'

He was the strongest man she'd ever known, yet

this town was his Achilles' heel. Everybody had one. But Clara had never suspected that a small seaside town could have such an effect on a powerful man.

'You'd think in a whole town,' said Jared with a frown, as though feeling the attack on his Achilles' tendon, 'there'd be one person willing to betray me for money.'

'That's the cynic in you talking.' She smiled wryly. 'You've always believed that every man has his price. But it's not true, Jared. There are some things that can't be bought.'

He laughed sardonically. 'If a reporter came down here with an open cheque someone would spill the beans.'

'Ah, but no reporter is aware that a story even exists here. And that tells me something very important.'

'Go on. Shatter me. What does it tell you?'

'That these people feel a great deal of loyalty to you. If not to you, then to your family or the Llewellyns.'

'Loyalty!' He looked at her cynically. 'Do me a favour!'

'I don't know precisely what happened here,' she continued. 'But it clearly rocked this little town on its heels the way the Profumo scandal rocked England. And you were at the centre of it.'

He looked at her through heavy eyelids and said nothing.

'It can't just have been your mother going to live with Owain. It must have been something more. Jared, I'm not brain-dead. Even I can see that something huge happened here. People file past constantly, stare and whisper, talk about you behind your back—'

'They always did,' he said quietly. 'That in itself is nothing new.'

'No. Okay. But if what happened is so very shocking, why has no one talked? It must be loyalty, Jared. There's simply no other feasible explanation.'

He looked out of the window in thoughtful silence. Clara wondered if he was considering the possibility. She hoped so. It would make such a difference to his feelings about the village if he was able to recognise the extraordinary loyalty they'd all shown him.

When they walked into the living room of the suite, Clara kicked her shoes off and sank with a sigh onto the couch. He joined her, stretching his shoulder muscles, but stopped halfway through with a groan as he saw the red light on the ivory telephone.

'Not more messages! I'm really not in the mood for business.'

'Take them after dinner,' she suggested.

'Good plan.' His legendary discipline was lapsing under the strain of all this. 'Speaking of which— where shall we eat?'

'I don't mind. Wherever you like.'

'I think we'd be best advised to eat here, actually. It's expensive, out of town and formal. Much less chance of bumping into any of the villagers, I think.'

After he had booked the table, Clara stretched out on the couch, purring, 'Oh, bliss! One whole hour with absolutely nothing to do…'

'Oh, I don't know,' he murmured, moving closer. 'I could think of something to keep us occupied…'

They took a shower together. The smoked glass cubicle steamed up as he slowly soaped her naked body inch by delicious inch, and their breathing grew as steamy as the doors until he pinned her against the wall and took her to seventh heaven.

In warm, loving silence they dressed together. Clara adjusted his tie, fastened his cufflinks. He zipped up the back of her long sexy red dress.

'You look stunning,' he murmured.

'So do you.'

'I almost wish we *could* bump into someone I once knew,' he drawled as they walked arm in arm to the lifts. 'Then I could show you off.'

'I tell you what—you show me off to your home town, and I'll take you to my old orphanage one day so I can show you off to Matron. How's that?'

'Just say the word, baby.'

She was smiling as she stepped into the lift with him. He'd been more than generous to her old orphanage. Every Christmas, crateloads of teddy bears arrived from Jared. He also sent them a handsome cheque every April. But there was little point in paying a visit to the place. Matron had long since retired, and so had everybody else she'd once known there.

But the villagers of Rhossana were all still here. The restaurant was packed with familiar faces, all waiting for Jared Blackheath and his famous girlfriend to make their entrance. Unfortunately, when he had rung down and booked a table for two, Jared had made a fatal error. The restaurant manager had immediately alerted the whole town, because there they were, sitting at every table, eyes glued to the door.

'Do you want to leave?' Clara asked quietly.

'No.' His face set with steely determination. 'If they want a show, I'll give them one to make their eyes drop out of their gossipy heads.' He beckoned the head waiter.

'Mr Blackheath, sir!' The head waiter practically fell over himself to bow. 'I never thought we'd greet you back at Rhossana, but—'

'Thank you,' Jared cut in coolly. 'But I'm in need of a stiff drink and some good food. I'd like to go straight to my table.'

'Of course, sir! The best table in the house...'

Everyone stared as they walked through the crowded restaurant to sit down, as they should have been able to predict, right at the back of the room where everyone could see them.

Jared was furious. But he seated Clara with cool self-assurance, took the seat opposite with an aura of charismatic power that made Clara smile admiringly, and looked about as unrattled as a sleepy panther.

'Bring me a double whisky on the rocks,' he ordered the head waiter.

'I'll have a gin and Slimline, please,' Clara said, looking forward to the first alcoholic drink she'd had since the wedding.

The head waiter departed.

'Forgive me if I don't lean towards you, darling,' Jared drawled when they were alone. 'But I have no intention of looking anything other than completely in control of everything, from the wine list to my sexy girlfriend.'

'That's okay. I'm not proud. I'll do the leaning.'

He laughed softly as she did so. 'Please do. The view is scintillating.'

Shivering with excitement, she felt his hot gaze drop to probe the dusky hollow between her breasts. She felt her nipples erect. It was only an hour since they'd made love in the shower. Clearly they were both aroused again. Pressure, she thought. It stimulates us both in more ways than one.

'It brings out the fighter in you, doesn't it?' she observed. 'To be cornered like this by so many people.'

'How do you think I got my scar? And you're no different, are you, Clara? You feel the determination to win just as much as I do tonight.'

'It's not really my fight.'

'Isn't it?' He studied her with shrewd certainty. 'You stand to lose a lot if this little trip to Wales goes wrong. There are an awful lot of emotional bombs lying around waiting to be either defused or to be blown up in our faces.'

'Oh, I think I can handle unexploded bombs. Why do you think I fell for you?'

He laughed under his breath and his eyes glittered vivid blue.

Their drinks arrived. They ordered. Clara chose grilled sole with a baked potato and green salad without dressing.

'And a bottle of Château Lafite.' Jared snapped the wine menu shut as though he were at the Paris Ritz, and Clara hid a smile. They wanted to see the legend living according to his image, and that was precisely what Jared was giving them.

The head waiter nearly expired with excitement. 'Oh, I hope we've still got some, Mr Blackheath! It's been so long since anyone ordered it. Not much call for Château Lafite down here, see...' He went hurrying off.

When they were alone, Clara said, 'It must be strange to be surrounded by Welsh voices again.'

'And the next question, no doubt, is why I speak with an English accent?'

'I just wondered, that's all.'

He studied her with narrowed eyes. 'I acquired it when I first arrived in London aged seventeen. I wanted to destroy all traces of my old self. That included the accent. So I got rid of it, pronto.'

'Did you go to evening classes?'

'No. I did it myself. Alone in my bedsit at nights. Listening to Radio Four and trying to copy each vowel sound. Pacing the floor, talking to myself until I was word-perfect. What determination!' He laughed, looking back into the past with self-recognition. 'My God, I was a driven man. I had no one. No friends, no supporters—just myself, my ambition and the occasional woman to keep me company on long winter nights.'

How little I really know him, she thought as she imagined the strength it must have taken to accomplish all that single-handedly. He'd been right when he'd said he wanted to destroy his old self. In many ways he was completely different from the teenager who had left Rhossana twenty years ago.

But Clara knew only too well how impossible it was to completely leave one's childhood identity behind. Perhaps it was for that reason that fate had brought Jared back here. He needed to get in touch with that long-forgotten, long-buried self. But why had he felt such an overriding need to destroy it…?

Their food arrived. Her grilled sole didn't look half as good as his duck *à l'orange* and his sauté potatoes.

'Of course,' Jared was saying as he finished his meal, 'there were moments when I did feel almost beaten. But I always managed to fight my way through and win in the end.'

'Single-handedly?'

'Always.'

'There were never any supporters? Not one?'

'Not really.' He ran a long finger over the rim of his wine glass. 'I guess when you're used to handling everything alone, it becomes force of habit.'

'Is that why you never told anyone about your past?' she asked softly.

His gaze darted up to study her for a long moment.

'Excuse me, sir, madam.' The head waiter swished up to their table without warning. 'A courier has arrived with an urgent message for Miss Maye. He refuses to leave until he has personally delivered the message into her hands. Shall I send him in or—?'

'No.' Clara got to her feet, pale and excited as she realised the message must be from Mitch, and that she might have won the part of Rachel after all. Even if she had to turn it down because of Susie's coma, and there was no guarantee she would come out of it, in spite of what the doctor said—it was still an accolade to have won the role. 'I'll come out to him. Is he in Reception?'

'I'll come with you.' Jared stood up, uncoiling to his full height of six foot six.

Everyone watched as he put his hand possessively beneath Clara's elbow and together they strode across the crowded restaurant. Heads turned, people whispered. Clara recognised several faces from around town, too. People who'd been pointed out to her by Jared, though she could not remember their names. The butcher's son and his plump wife. The hospital orderly and his long-haired girlfriend.

Suddenly Gwyneth Jones was getting up from her table and smiling at them. The silver low-cut evening dress was too tight, and she wore too much make-up, but her natural prettiness shone through.

'Jared?' Gwyneth's voice was breathless as she stood directly in their path. 'I'm sorry to intrude, but I just wanted to say hello.'

Smiling tightly, Jared replied, 'Hello. Excuse me, but I'm in rather a hurry…' Striding past her, he went out of the dining room, keeping a tight hold on Clara's elbow.

Across the foyer, Clara saw a tall young man in motorcycle leathers. He held a zip-up package in one hand. But before they could reach him Gwyneth Jones caught Jared's arm, and Jared—not realising who it was—turned with an unguarded frown.

'I don't just want to say hello.' Gwyneth's face was flushed. 'I want to say I'm sorry. Sorry for the way I treated you when we were children. We all are. We always have been, ever since—'

'We really are in a hurry—'

'I was so young, Jared!'

'Yes, I do understand, but—'

'And your father's suicide was—'

'We have to go!' Jared bit out hoarsely, and strode forward with Clara.

She moved like a robot. Shock reflected in her eyes. Jared's fingers bit into her arm as he led her across the chandeliered foyer and everything seemed to have gone into slow motion. Suicide! The word kept hammering in her mind. Of course, why hadn't she realised it before? Everything fell into place and made perfect sense now. The chance remarks, the little clues, were all adding up to make her shiver with horror.

'You're the courier?' Jared stopped in the centre of the foyer.

'Yup. And you're Jared Blackheath. I don't need to ask if this is the gorgeous Miss Clara Maye!' He grinned at her admiringly. 'Seen you on the telly. Loved you as Jezebel Whitney.'

'Just give her the damned package!' Jared was furious with him for flirting so openly with Clara.

'Sorry.' The courier fumbled in his zip-up bag, handed Clara a form to sign and then the package.

'We'll take it straight up to our suite,' Jared muttered as soon as she had the slim white envelope in her hands, and without another word led her over to the lifts.

They rode up in tense silence. She was too stunned to even open the envelope, clutching it in nerveless fingers, all thought of Rachel forgotten.

'Stop staring at me!' Jared bit out under his breath,

only too well aware of the bombshell that had been dropped. 'Open the damned envelope!'

Automatically, she did. Scanning the letter as the lift stopped at their floor, she said, 'It's from Mitch. He's been ringing and leaving messages here all day.'

'Damn it…how was I to know?'

'Oh, Jared…' Her voice trembled with excitement. 'I've got a recall for the part of Rachel. I'm in the last three. It's nearly mine. I can't believe it.'

'When's the recall?'

Her excitement died. 'Tomorrow, midday, in London.'

'What are you going to do?' He strode to the doors of their suite, unlocking them and ushering her in.

Shellshocked, she walked into the living room like a beautiful blonde ghost. Her mind was racing in twenty different directions at once. Now that the role was within her grasp she was faced with the choice she had not wanted to make. But deep inside she knew what it would be: Susie.

'You don't have much time to make a decision.' He was pale too, and his movements were jerky, on edge.

She tried to think. 'A recall…tomorrow…'

'Perhaps a brandy might help,' he said suddenly, and went to the drinks cabinet, looking much more in control apart from the white-knuckled fingers as he unscrewed two miniatures.

That was when she realised he was as disorientated as she was.

'Darling?' she asked huskily. 'Are you all right?'

'Fine!'

But he was far from fine. This was what he'd been afraid of all along. That someone would one day come up to him in public and blurt it out.

'A recall is just another test, isn't it?' His hand shook as he poured the brandies.

'They might want to shoot a multiple character scene. Maybe put me together with the hero, see how the chemistry works.'

'Essential stuff?'

'They can't cast me without it.'

'Well, you can still go. Take my helicopter. That'll get you to London and back in no time.'

'Yes...' Conversation sounded so normal, but it wasn't. They were both just trying to make it look normal because neither of them wanted to say that word. And now she knew what the house had whispered as the storm raged over the bay. Now she knew why he hid his feelings from her, refused to talk about it, couldn't bear to be reminded of it.

'It's your Hamlet,' Jared said roughly.

She managed a wan smile.

'Congratulations, darling.' He strode to her, handed her the glass of brandy and raised his own to his lips. 'I see an award nomination in the future.'

'I haven't even got the part yet. There are never any guarantees until the contracts are signed.'

'Of course.' He drained his glass and did not look at her. 'But I'm very pleased for you, nonetheless.'

He was trying to detract attention from the burning issue. People always talked too much when they were running inside themselves. Talked too much, did too much, put on too strong a front and prayed that no

one would notice the Achilles' heel which had been
so suddenly and brutally exposed.

'So what will you do?' he demanded, before the
conversation could move towards what they really
wanted to talk about.

Clara stared for a second, then shook her head.
'You know how much I want the part. How hard I've
worked for it. Rehearsing endlessly, memorising
every single relevant piece of the script.'

'I remember you sectioning up that monologue.
You stuck one piece on the fridge. Another on the
bedside table. Even one on the inside door of the
shower.'

Tears stung her eyes as she laughed. 'I was so determined to get it right. To change my career for ever
and earn some serious respect.'

'You can go for this test, Clara. I'll stay with Susie.
I'll keep watch for you.'

'And if the doctor is wrong?' she whispered. 'If
she dies?'

Their eyes met and held in mutual pain. He looked
away first.

They both knew it was impossible. No step up the
career ladder was more important than a friend who
was virtually a sister. Clara couldn't desert her. It was
still possible, in spite of the good news today, that she
might die. And if she did the long term repercussions
for Clara would be terrible.

'I'd never forgive myself.' She shook her blonde
head with a pained expression. 'If I got the part, I'd
always know how I got it, by abandoning Susie. I'd

turn against the part. I might even destroy any hope I have of playing it well.'

'Yes…' he said deeply, staring.

Again, their eyes met. This time he didn't look away. This time his gaze held hers and she saw the darkness in them as he stopped, finally, running inside, and found the courage to just stand still as the lines of deep trust began to open up between them through his eyes.

'Death is too terrible, Jared,' she said when he remained silent. 'The repercussions last for ever. That's why it's so important to get everything right if and when it does touch your shoulder.'

'Yes,' he said again, still staring. 'It shatters lives, rewrites history and obliterates every fixed point on the map. If you don't handle this absolutely right, you'll live to regret it.'

There was a brief silence.

Then he said in a voice which broke, 'I know I did.'

CHAPTER EIGHT

TEARS sprang to Jared's eyes. He turned his back on Clara.

'Darling…' she said huskily, moving towards him.

'No!' He held up a strong hand, determined not to be comforted, as though his vulnerability was a crime, as though it made him less of a man, summoning his fierce drive not to break down or show weakness.

Breathing hard, he took the time he needed to pull his formidable façade back into place. But he kept his back to her the whole time and would not look around. He'd always been so determined to fight his demons alone. As he had said earlier, it was force of habit and old habits died very hard indeed.

Finally he said, 'I thought I might be able to keep this hidden for ever. It's not that I've ever been ashamed of my father's decision. It's more a question of wanting to preserve his dignity the best way I can. Silence, in my opinion, is the only intelligent option. But that silence has been broken now…' He stopped talking, drawing a deep breath, and she realised the enormous effort he was making to try and end the silence of a lifetime.

'You don't have to talk about it if you really don't want to,' she said softly.

'There's no point in keeping up the charade. Gwyneth's little bombshell has been dropped. It can't be undropped, much as I'd like it to be. But I don't want to talk about how he did it or—'

'I understand.'

'Do you? I hope so. You looked so shocked when Gwyneth blurted it out downstairs. I thought—'

'If I was shocked, it's because I never imagined suicide. In fact, I never connected your fear of the past with your father. I was too busy focusing on your mother.'

'Oh, everyone was always too busy focusing on her.' He gave a bitter smile. 'My father got swept under the carpet like a broken-down piece of old junk. He was just a cuckold. A fool. A worthless idiot whose wife had left—'

'No, Jared.' she said urgently, putting a hand on his arm. 'You mustn't think that way!'

'It's not how I think!' he bit out hoarsely, swinging round to her, his face so fierce with pent-up emotion that she felt the full impact of his rage and pain, all of it locked in that isolated heart for so long and suddenly unleashed. 'I've never seen my father that way! Never! He was a fantastic man! The best father I could have had!'

He looked away as soon as he'd spoken. He ran a hand over his eyes as though it hurt him just to talk about his father. But he had to talk about him. And she had to help him. No matter what he said about not wanting to discuss the suicide—he needed badly to do so.

Quickly, she asked, 'What was his name?'

'Bryn. Bryn Blackheath. He was tall, good-looking and had the kind of easy charm the Welsh are famous for. I understand he was a great success with women. All the local girls were in love with him when he was a young man. He had a good job at Llewellyn's. He was a hod-carrier.' He gave a brief shrug. 'Not exactly glamorous, but it paid very well. And he was enormously popular with his male friends. Always drinking at the pub with his buddies. Singing and telling stories and being the life and soul of Rhossana. Until *she* came...' His eyes darkened and his tone grew harsh. 'She was beautiful, then. Nineteen years old and admired by everyone. The perfect match for Bryn. Their passion flared like a jet-propelled rocket. It got them to the altar in double-quick time, said their marriage vows for them and gave birth to me.'

'Did Lily tell you all this? Afterwards or—?'

'I can't remember how I know it. I feel as though I've always known it. Or rather...*he* knew it. The boy I used to be. I believed for so long that I wasn't that boy, that I'd never be him again.' His voice roughened. 'But I think now maybe I was wrong...or this wouldn't hurt so damned much.'

She touched the scar on his hard cheek with gentle fingers. 'If I opened this old wound it would hurt again.'

He looked into her eyes.

'You're not sixteen, as you were when you got this scar. And you're not in a street-fight in Cardiff with a drunk sailor trying to steal your girl.'

'No,' he said thickly, 'but I am in Rhossana and they're all waiting to see me crack. I mustn't crack. Don't let me crack. Don't—'

'Who, you?' she said with a loving smile. 'That'll be the day.'

He smiled tautly, but a second later his eyes moved back to those dark and bitter memories.

'They probably don't realise how much they're getting to you,' she said quickly. 'People rarely do. Particularly when the object of their fascination is such a powerful individual.'

'Rhossana's most famous son!' he said bitterly.

'Try to understand how they must feel about you, darling. To me, you're just Jared. To them—you must seem like some kind of sacred monster.'

He gave a hollow laugh.

'And isn't that what all this has made you? The scandal, the tragedy and then the leap to international fame. Just why have they never betrayed you?'

'What does that have to do with creating a sacred monster?'

'It has this to do with it, Jared: you must never kill your sacred monster. You must protect it.'

He was silent, black brows drawing in a frown as he considered what she'd said. To him, his fame was a fortress designed to protect him. But, to the villagers, it must have made him seem awe-inspiring.

'I wish they could appreciate,' he said, 'how deep my father's death went with me. Not just his death. The whole thing. My mother's affair, the way she flaunted herself with Owain, playing Lady of the Manor and in doing so—destroying my father.'

'I'm sure they do understand. They just don't know how to communicate it.'

'My father wasn't the only one who was destroyed,

Clara,' he said thickly. 'A part of me died with him. I felt it die. I saw it die. It was as though the boy I'd been suddenly disappeared, and this new me—the strong, ambitious boy—took his place.'

She understood immediately and knew it was wholly accurate, because she had changed dramatically too when her own parents had died in the fire.

'Did it really start then?' she asked.

He was unsurprised that she understood. He just glanced at her as he spoke, almost as though he'd always known that she was the one, the only one who would ever hear this and understand.

'It was the only way I could deal with what had happened. I couldn't tolerate that other self. The scared, angry boy who kicked and punched anyone who laughed at him. The boy with no friends. The boy with no future and a terrible past. When my father died I just couldn't tolerate being that boy any more. I had to become someone else.'

'Maybe,' she suggested softly, 'it had more to do with the fact that it was over?'

'What was over?'

'The whole thing, Jared. The affair, the arguments, the scandal. When your father died it ended everything for ever. A new era began. Maybe that's what you felt die.'

He was suddenly incapable of speech, staring at her.

'Have you ever heard the phrase "freed by trauma?"' she asked gently. 'Darling, sometimes it takes a tragedy to free people from an intolerable situation.'

'And what about my father?' he demanded. 'What about his freedom? He lost his life over this! How am I to forgive them for that? They destroyed his self-esteem, his whole identity, his belief in his place in the world. Who wouldn't contemplate death under those circumstances?'

Huskily, she said, 'You?'

Emotions flickered across his face. It just showed how important it was to talk these things through with someone who really loved you, Clara thought. Nobody had ever answered the questions he needed to ask because he had never asked them. And now, as he began to break the isolation he had lived with all his life, he was able to leave his fortress and look at the world outside with new eyes.

It was clearly very different from the world he had always believed lay beyond the parapets and battlements and moat. His strength had isolated him as much as it had protected him. But, with Clara, he had found a way out, and now he began truly accepting the help she was only too glad to give.

He said, 'I must admit that I've often felt very angry with him for doing it. I guess I just couldn't bring myself to look at that anger. It seemed so disloyal.'

'We all feel ambivalent emotions when someone close to us dies—'

'I don't think I can talk about it any more,' he cut in, his voice raw and unsteady.

'Darling, you'll feel so much better if—'

'I can't! Don't ask again!'

She fell silent as she saw the fear leap in his eyes. He reacted like a wounded animal every time she went near that memory. But it was like the thorn in the lion's paw: it had to come out. In his rage and pain he lashed out without realising that it was the thorn which was causing it all.

'I'll abide by any decision you make,' she said quietly. 'But I think you'd prefer to tell me privately rather than risk another incident like tonight.'

He closed his eyes and drew a harsh breath. There was a long silence. The clock on the mantelpiece ticked softly. Slowly, Jared walked over to the drinks cabinet to refill his glass. He concentrated on opening the miniature bottle, but halfway through he dropped it and leaned his hands on the table in front of him, breathing harshly.

'My father died in the great hall of the Manor.'

She'd thought she would feel horror when she finally heard him say it, but she felt only relief that it was finally over, and, as she thought that, she saw the boy in Jared step out from the shadows of the powerful adult he had become, and she knew he had turned some momentous corner towards recovery.

'It was summer,' he said deeply. 'Everyone was at the fête on the village green. I'd arranged to meet my father there because of course I had no other friends to meet, only him. My mother arrived in Owain's swanky Bentley. I hated her because she was dressed up like a Chanel model and sashaying around on his arm. But most of all I hated her because my father hadn't arrived. I was sure it was because of her.'

'Did she try to talk to you?'

'No, she didn't even see me. To be fair to her, I didn't want her to see me. Not like that. Not with everyone watching. I hung back from the main crowd and after an hour or so I went looking for Da.'

Ah, she thought, Da. So that was what his nightmare had been all about. His voice was even beginning to take on a faint Welsh lilt as he talked. The mention of 'Da' instead of 'my father' showed how great the inner corner he was turning really was.

'I went to the cottage, the pub—all the usual haunts—but I couldn't find him anywhere. I didn't want to go back to the fête, so I went for a walk. It was a beautiful day. Very hot, bright blue sky—I remember it so vividly. Even down to the wild strawberries I picked and ate on the way. Then suddenly I saw the Manor, rising up above the hedgerows, and I thought—I wonder if he's there?'

'You hadn't meant to make your way there, then?'

'The Manor was the last place I would have looked for him. But when I saw it I just had a feeling he was there. I remember thinking I'd be safe, even if I didn't find him, because nobody else would be there. They were all at the fête, including the staff.'

'You saw them there?'

'Yes…but, just to make sure, I climbed the wall so no one would see me. I needn't have worried. The front doors were ajar. And as I walked across the manicured lawns I began to feel scared. I felt as though the house was waiting for me. Whispering to me, almost, but I was only eight and I told myself it was the breeze, not the house.'

She moved closer, eyes wide. 'Yes, I felt that. The day you came to get me. I heard the whispers—from the house. Uncanny…'

He knew her well enough to know she told the truth. He also knew that she'd described his own feelings, as though she'd been in his eight-year-old's shoes that day, the day he'd found his father.

And as she looked into his eyes she saw the final barrier lift and the real Jared show himself: a man of great seriousness and depth who had only just recognised the enormity of his love for her. He was meant to tell her this. He felt the hand of destiny at the same moment she did, and she shivered as it touched her shoulder, very softly, from a long way away, just as the house had whispered its long-kept secrets to her, as it had to him on that summer afternoon thirty years ago.

'It was the house, then,' he said deeply. 'I always believed it was.'

'They say the feelings of the dead can stay in a house for centuries.'

'But whose feelings, Clara? His or mine?'

'Everybody's. That house was the epicentre of the tragedy from the beginning.'

He nodded. 'There was never anywhere else. Everything was linked to the Manor from the start of the affair until the day of my father's death. The day I found Da, I stood on the steps without moving for a long time. The doors were ajar...' his voice slurred '...but I had a gut instinct. I was only eight, so I imagined there were monsters in the hall, waiting for me. Then I told myself not to be weak. I was Bryn Blackheath's son and I wasn't afraid of monsters, so I summoned all my courage and opened the door. I saw him at once.'

Clara touched his hand, unable to speak.

'I sat on the floor and tried to think what to do. Then I heard the car in the drive and a second later my mother was standing in the doorway, screaming.'

'Was she alone?' Clara asked huskily.

'No, the fête had ended and Owain had driven her home. He was standing just behind her and Jones the chauffeur was there, too.'

'Jones…that wouldn't be a relation of—?'

'Gwyneth. Yes. He was her father. That's how she found out the full story and spread it around the class.'

'The picture she drew on the blackboard…'

'Gruesome, yes. But she must have been in a state of shock, too. I think the whole town was. I didn't realise that until today, but now I see how they must all have felt.' He cleared his throat, frowning. 'It was the conversation with you, about loyalty, that made me see it. What you said about the Profumo scandal affecting everyone in the country…in many ways you hit the nail on the head with that one. Everyone in Rhossana went through the tragedy of Bryn Blackheath's death. It hurt us all.'

'But you were the figurehead, Jared,' she said at once, for she didn't want him to lose sight of how much greater his suffering had been than any other person's, either in his family or in this town. His whole life and character had been shaped by these forces. 'You were the one at the centre of it all along. That's why you felt it so deeply and for so many years. Although everyone else did suffer, you were just a child. Lily's husband died. Owain's rival died.

The town lost a well-loved friend…but *you* lost your father.'

He drew an uneven breath. 'I think in many ways it went so deep that I just refused to look at it. That's why I made sure that everything changed from that moment on. It was the only way to deal with it. The only way to survive.'

Clara kissed him tenderly. 'You survived magnificently, darling. You made the right decisions, even though you were only eight.'

'But did I?' He frowned thoughtfully. 'If I did, why has coming back here affected me so much?'

'That's only natural. When you left here you were seventeen, and still driven by the need to become wealthy, successful and famous. But that was twenty years ago, and look at you now. It's just time for fate to bring you back to the place where it all started.'

He studied her for a moment. 'I think the after-shocks of the tragedy are responsible, too.'

She smiled and kissed him. 'Tell me about the aftershocks.'

'I think I'd like another brandy first!' He groaned, laughing. 'Going down Memory Lane isn't as bad as I thought it'd be, but it's still draining and depressing!'

He poured them each a small brandy. Clara put the kettle on and made some coffee too. While the odd brandy was easing the stress for Jared in finally making his confession, she knew it was best if he stayed reasonably clear-headed.

'There are a couple of biscuits here, too,' she told him as he sank wearily onto the couch.

'I'll eat them both,' he drawled, laughing as he put

his feet up on the coffee table. She settled down beside him, curling her feet up beneath her and sipping the brandy he handed her.

'Well,' he said, stretching, 'after they found Da, I ran off. I went to a cave under the cliffs and hid there for a long time—the whole village formed search parties. Dai Williams's father and his friends found me.'

'Dai Williams...' She searched her memory. 'Oh, yes, the vicar's son. He's a doctor now, at the hospital. He walked past the room once or twice to stare at you.'

'Da's funeral was a couple of days later and my mother moved out of the Manor.'

'She left Owain after the funeral?'

'No, she moved out of the Manor directly after Da's death. But it wasn't official until after the funeral. That's when she had all her possessions moved back into the cottage to live with me. I refused pointblank to move into the Manor.'

'I don't blame you.' Clara sipped her coffee and surreptitiously offered him his cup, too, which he took along with both biscuits.

'Afterwards no one ever discussed it with me, Clara. The kids at school just stared at me as though I was a freak. The villagers kept treating me as an object of pity. I hated it. I hated being me. I hated having to see them all, year after year...'

She touched his hand with love and understanding. 'A death like that is too horrible for most people to handle, darling. They've protected you, stayed silent and showed unwavering loyalty for thirty years. And for ten of those years you weren't famous. Or rich.

Or newsworthy. Or powerful. Their loyalty is to you—not your success.'

He heaved a heavy sigh, studying the coffee cup as he put it down on the table. 'I've always been afraid someone would sell the story. I guess I misjudged them all terribly. I misjudged my mother, too...'

'Did you, darling?' she asked as he sat back against the warmth of the couch.

'I hated her,' he said thickly. 'As I grew up—surrounded by memories of my dead father—I hated her so bitterly I frequently couldn't bring myself to speak to her. I remember when Owain moved away and remarried. I remember that she cried, endlessly, for months because she'd lost both the men she loved in one fell swoop.

'And how do you feel about her now?'

'I've forgiven her, but I'll never feel like running into her arms and hugging her,' he said frankly. 'Feelings that deep don't go away. They just fade with time. She did her best to make it up to me but the damage was irreparable. I left home as soon as I was seventeen. I only needed one year's work after leaving school to save enough to get me to London. She tried to stop me, saying I was crazy to think I'd be a success. So I didn't bother to leave a forwarding address. And I didn't contact her again for five years.'

She nodded slowly. 'Well, that explains everything. I always found your relationship strange. The distance between you, the rare visits, and the way you'd suddenly join forces against me if I asked too many questions.'

'Perhaps now you can understand why I shied away

from those questions?' he asked softly, putting a hand over hers.

'Completely.' She leaned over to kiss him.

'And why I reacted as I did at Susie's wedding?'

'Oh, that's as clear as crystal to me now!' She slid her arms around his chest and he held her close as she kissed his throat, buried her face in his neck. 'What a terrible day that must have been for you! But how glad I am that it happened!'

'Me too,' he confessed huskily, kissing the top of her head. 'I'd known from the minute Susie fell in love with Gareth that this was on the cards. Every step she took closer to the altar brought me one step closer to Owain Llewellyn.'

'And one step closer to the Manor.'

'It was a nightmare sitting next to him at the Ritz. When he started to make that speech I just knew what he was going to say. I *knew* it. I felt so powerless.'

She kissed his tough cheek. 'I wonder what Owain was thinking when he made that speech. It can't have been easy.'

'We'll never know. Although I suspect he was thinking a little about my mother. He did genuinely love her. And I have a strong feeling they'll get back together again.'

Drawing back to look at him, she smiled. 'I've wondered about that!'

'Well, it does look as though it's going to happen,' he said wryly. 'In fact, it may already have happened. Remember I told you that when I rang my mother with news of Susie's wedding, she didn't seem surprised.'

'Oh, yes—you said she almost seemed to know about it before you did.'

'One guess who told her,' he said with a cynical laugh.

She studied his face carefully. 'And how do you feel about that?'

He was silent for a moment, then eventually said, 'I can't stand in their way. I wouldn't have tried at any stage. Owain was right when he said I wasn't the only one who had suffered. They did suffer, too. And if they deserved punishment, they've certainly had their fill.'

'Do you forgive them, though?'

He gave a harsh sigh and nodded. 'Yes...I forgive them. Both of them. It's been a long time, Clara. And my father is with me for the rest of my life, no matter what they say or do.'

Just then the telephone rang.

'That,' said Jared, 'can only be the hospital.' He got to his feet and strode to the phone while Clara watched in an agony of fear in case it was bad news.

'Yes?' Jared answered. There was a burst of sound from the earpiece. 'What! You're kidding! Oh, thank God!'

Clara's heart flew fast with hope as she saw the light blaze in his eyes and a smile transform his face.

'But that means she could wake up at any minute!' Jared was saying. 'Did the doctor tell you that? Definitely? We'll be there in ten minutes' flat!'

She leapt to her feet and ran to him. 'What's happened?'

He put the phone down, excited. 'Her eyes are

moving. Her mouth is moving. They think she's going to wake up. This is it. Sleeping Beauty's maybe just about to open her eyes and say hello!'

CHAPTER NINE

TEN minutes later, the limousine screeched to a halt outside the hospital. Jared leapt out with Clara, and they ran all the way to Intensive Care. They looked so out of place, he in a formal black evening suit, she in a long red gown.

'Don't go in!' Gareth was waiting for them and pointed hurriedly to the doctor and three nurses who were currently leaning over Susie. She was still asleep, but the machines rattled more noisily than ever before, showing improvement in all vital signs.

'She's not awake yet?' Clara asked breathlessly.

'No,' Gareth replied. 'I rang you as soon as they took over. It was all very quick, very professional. They shooed me out and I was so excited I had to tell someone! I just know Susie's on the mend. I can feel it. She's going to wake up. Tonight, maybe tomorrow. But some time soon.'

'I think you're right.' Jared peered through the glass room at the sleeping Susie. 'Let's hope the—'

Suddenly, the nurses and doctor exited in a flurry of white coats, pale blue dresses and clipboards.

'Is something wrong?' Jared demanded.

'On the contrary.' The doctor clicked his pen and put it back in the breast pocket of his white coat. 'Everything looks extremely promising. But don't get your hopes up yet.'

'Can we go back in?' asked Gareth.

'Yes,' smiled the doctor, 'and keep talking to her.'

They went into the room. Clara sank down at Susie's bedside. Jared stood behind her chair, long hands sliding onto Clara's shoulders, while Gareth took the chair on the other side of the bed.

'Darling, wake up.' Gareth took Susie's hand and began talking urgently. 'We're all here.'

'Jared and I rushed over here from the hotel.' Clara held her other hand. 'We look rather silly—all dressed up for a party, and you're the star guest!'

'They make a great couple,' Gareth agreed. 'Just think—if you wake up, you might be able to persuade them to get married!'

Susie's eyelids moved. They all gasped and leaned forward, holding their collective breath until it became clear that Susie was not going to wake up just yet.

'Wow!' breathed Gareth, staring at Susie. 'That had an effect!'

Clara tensed, aware that Jared had gone very still and silent all of a sudden. He hated weddings, marriage—and for good reasons. Just because he'd finally unburdened his soul to her with that confession it didn't mean his feelings about marriage would change.

'Say it again,' Gareth whispered, desperate for anything that might wake Susie up. 'Only say it yourselves this time, and with lots of feeling.'

Clara looked at Jared. His face was tough, unreadable.

'Please!' urged Gareth on a hoarse whisper. 'If you

really don't want to get married for real afterwards, at least say it to make her wake up!'

Jared's dark eyes turned to Susie, then to Clara. He stared at her in absolute silence for a long time. What must he be thinking? she wondered, but of course she knew. He didn't want to be a husband. He was afraid that if he ever became some woman's husband he would end up cuckolded, humiliated and with his brilliantly constructed 'new' identity in ruins. He had very good reason to fear that because of his father's terrible experience. But Clara was not Lily. They had not met as unsuited teenagers. And Clara knew their marriage would not end up as his parents' marriage had. It was just that she could not prove that to him without actually marrying him. And he would never marry her until she did prove it.

'Susie.' Jared suddenly seemed to reach a private decision without consulting Clara. 'It's true.'

Breathless, Clara stared up at him in stunned silence. He did not meet her eyes.

'Watching you and Gareth get married has changed my mind,' Jared said deeply, making Clara's heart beat faster with incredulous hope until he continued with, 'I haven't actually asked Clara to marry me yet, and I doubt if I will just yet.' Her heart plummeted as he said that, but she managed to remain smiling—just—as he went on. 'At least, not until I've had time to think things through away from Wales. But I am beginning to look at marriage with different eyes. And I have you to thank for that, Susie. Please wake up soon so I can tell you how you've changed everything for me.'

It was a compromise, and a clever one at that. He hadn't lied to Susie, or even to Clara. He'd just found a route out of a difficult situation, and, although Clara's heart sank as she saw the clever side-stepping, she nevertheless admired him for it. At least he had not lied blatantly. Somehow that was important to her.

Gareth took the compromise and embroidered heavily upon it. 'You see, Susie? If you don't wake up, Jared won't be able to discuss it with you and then Clara might never get married!'

She could have slapped him. Feeling a fool, she had to sit there with a tense smile, trying not to show how rattled she was while she helped these two men to wake her best friend without once discussing the feelings they had both just helped to hurt.

'Everything's going to be all right now, Susie,' Jared was saying. 'All you have to do is wake up.'

'That's right,' Clara said through gritted teeth. 'Jared and I are going to be very happy, and we want you to share our happiness by waking up.'

But she didn't.

Time ticked slowly on. It was four in the morning, then five.

'All our problems are solved now.' Gareth was still excited by the belief that she'd wake up any minute now. 'When Clara and Jared are married, we'll be able to make up foursomes with them all the time!'

Susie's eyelids flickered again at five-fifteen. They all leaned forward again, breathless.

'She's got to wake up!' Gareth whispered, clutching her hand. 'Please, God, let her wake—'

Suddenly the eyelids flickered open. Susie blinked

once, twice. They were all incapable of movement, staring at her open-mouthed. She glanced round slowly at them all.

'Susie?' Clara whispered in shocked disbelief.

'Hello...' Susie said with a weak smile.

Once the rush of tears and laughter was over, Susie was moved to an observation ward. The doctors pronounced her well enough for normal hospital life but wanted to run tests, keep an eye on her and monitor her recovery inch by inch. They also didn't want her overtired. So, although they let Jared, Clara and Gareth stay for an hour after she woke up, they eventually ordered them home.

'Mrs Llewellyn is now on the road to recovery,' the doctor told them after shooing them all out into the corridor. 'Her other injuries are coming along and will be healed soon. Obviously the broken leg and fractured skull will take longer, but I don't anticipate any problems for her. She should be back to normal within three months.'

'Just as beautiful and agile as she was before the accident?' asked Gareth anxiously.

'Possibly even more so. A brush with death tends to give a new lease of life in the long run. Meanwhile, however, I want to make sure that there are no relapses. She's to have complete bed-rest for the next few days. That means no visitors except at normal times.'

'But I've been seeing her all day every—' Gareth began.

'As for you, Mr Llewellyn, I want you to go

straight home to bed, get plenty of sleep and do not return until eleven tomorrow morning.'

'But, Doctor, I—'

'No arguments. I don't want you to have a nervous breakdown.'

'But—'

'I'll give you a lift home, Gareth,' Jared intervened suddenly.

Clara did a double-take. 'A lift with Harrison?'

'No.' Jared took care not to look at her, and she knew it wouldn't have done any good if he had looked at her, because his eyes were unreadable.

'We'll both see him home. Harrison can drive.'

Astonished, she walked along beside him to the hospital exit, incapable of speech. Didn't he realise they would be dropping Gareth at the Manor? Now that she knew the full extent of what had happened in that old house, she couldn't quite believe Jared was ready to go there so soon. But what choice did she have? He clearly wanted to give Gareth a lift home, and she wondered briefly, as they left the hospital building, if he just wanted to postpone being alone with her. That conversation about marriage must have upset him, as it had her. He might very well just be trying to avoid talking about it privately with her.

Dawn had fully broken as they walked out into the open air. Gold light streaked the sky, a faint mist gave the morning a fresh scent and the sea, just visible in the distance, was clean blue as it broke gently on the dark rocks of Rhossana Bay.

'Oh, no!' Gareth checked his jeans pockets as the limousine slid up beside them. 'I left my mobile

phone in there. Shan't be a sec...' He sped off in his
trainers back into the hospital building.

Jared's dark blue eyes met Clara's. He gave a de-
fensive smile. 'What are you staring at?'

'Darling...' She bit her lip, wondering how to
phrase it. 'I do understand that you only wanted to
help Susie wake up. I won't hold you to anything you
said about marriage. I just—'

'Let's not discuss that right now,' he said thickly,
and looked away.

She knew better than to argue with him when he
used that tone. It always meant he would become angry if pushed. And the reason was that he refused
point-blank to confront or discuss emotions he was
not ready to deal with. It meant he had not yet reached
a decision. That was what it meant, she thought, heart
thudding faster. And if he hadn't reached a decision
yet...

Her breath caught. Was he seriously considering
marriage? It wasn't possible! She was scared to believe it in case it wasn't true, because if it wasn't true
then she'd build up false hopes only to have them
dashed—which would be too painful to bear.

Their eyes collided, broke apart. She felt her heart
race and her stomach clench with excitement, fear,
love...

Talk about something else! she thought in a panic.
And for heaven's sake think about something else.
Don't start having romantic daydreams about him going down on one knee and proposing marriage, because it's too fantastic to dream of, too dangerous
to pretend.

Remembering that they were going to the Manor, she heard her shaky voice say, 'Are you sure you want to go to the Manor?'

Jared looked down at her briefly. He was wary too. Excitement and some other indefinable emotion glittered in the back of his eyes. 'Why not?' he demanded, and his voice was rough.

'It's still so fresh in your mind, darling. I know you may think you can look through those double doors again and cope with it, but—'

'I want to look at it. I want to walk up the steps. I want to go in.'

'Inside? You mean inside—you don't mean inside the—?'

'Inside the hall, Clara.'

That stopped her excitement about the possibility of marriage in its tracks. She could not believe he seriously meant to go into that hall so soon after his first conversation about it in a lifetime—a whole lifetime. He was motionless, not looking at her. A cool breeze blew strands of black hair back from his forehead. He looked out across the grey rooftops towards the distant sea.

A seagull cried in the crisp morning air. Other than that there was silence. The village was still asleep and would not stir for at least an hour. Perhaps that was just as well, she thought, for Jared must have no witnesses to this, his first real visit to the Manor. If he really meant to do it, that was. And she could scarcely believe he did.

But what if he really was ready? And some instinct told her that he might just be ready. Maybe he'd been

ready for some time. The fact that she was the first
person ever to hear his whole tragic story should have
been clue enough as to how ready he had been when
he did finally tell her. They'd been living together for
two years, after all. Jared must have thought many
times about telling her during those two years. It was
just that he'd needed that one last nudge before he
finally made his confession—the nudge which had
come in the form of this enforced and very much surprise visit to Rhossana Bay.

Eventually, she said, 'You need to be sure.'

'Well, I'm not.' He gave a cool laugh. 'Not completely. It could be a mistake. But I don't feel it is.'

'You've only just broken the silence of decades,
Jared. Don't rush yourself. You might need more time
than you think.'

He studied the distant sea. 'I don't think I do. I no
longer feel the way I did about it. The house, the hall,
the whole thing. Something's changed. Something's...' His eyes narrowed thoughtfully. 'Something's...different.'

'You've been up all night. That may be all that's
different.'

'Hey, I'm thirty-seven years old.' He looked round
at her with eyes that blazed full of acceptance and
real forgiveness. 'I know how it feels to stay up all
night. But no matter how many times I've stayed up
late, being in love with you or reflecting privately on
the past...I never felt as free as I do right now.'

She was silent, respecting his words and not wish-
ing to intervene.

'It won't get much better than this,' he said deeply

after a moment. 'I feel as though a ten-ton weight has suddenly lifted off my neck. I can't understand why I carried it alone for so long. I want to face the house. I want to, Clara. I'd rather do it with you by my side, but if I have to face it alone—I will.'

She sighed lovingly and slid her arms around his strong waist. He smiled too, as though he understood how she felt and read the unspoken thoughts in her mind. Then he leaned back against the car, his arms around her. He looked years younger. Despite the lines etched around his eyes and mouth, he did look more free. His face seemed cleansed for ever—or was it finally?—of any trace of anger and bitterness. Just as the brightening dawn sky was cleansed by daylight of all its darkness.

'You know,' he said as he held her against his chest, 'you may have been right. Telling someone the whole story was probably what I needed.'

Her hands curled on his back. Yet she kept her voice steady, for all that she loved him more with each passing minute than she had ever thought she could love another human being. 'Let's reserve judgement until you see the house again. Until you step into that hallway.' In silence, she drew back to study his face, worried for him. He'd sounded so sure, so confident that he was right to do this so quickly. But what would happen if he was wrong?

'Okay,' she said softly. 'Whatever you want to do, I'll stand by you and your decision—just as I have all along.'

'You'll come in with me?'

'Of course.'

He was silent for a moment, studying her, his face very serious and his eyes filled with love. Then he bent his head to kiss her. The heat of his lips was sweetly at odds with the cold morning air surrounding them, and Clara wrapped her arms around him, kissing him back with tender passion as they locked into their loving embrace. Kissing in the car park at dawn, still in evening clothes, they looked precisely what they were: a couple in love who had just stayed up all night together.

'Got it!' Gareth came racing out of the hospital.

Startled, they broke off the kiss to look round. Jared grimaced, Clara's eyes flicked to his, and they smiled in private understanding of just how intrusive Gareth had inadvertently been.

As they drove away minutes later, Clara's hand nestled in Jared's and she thought about marriage with deep longing. It was sometimes so hard to stay quiet when your feelings were bubbling to the surface. She was so sure that he had begun to consider marriage, but what if she was wrong? And even if she was right, she had no business intervening in his private thought processes. If he really *had* begun to change his feelings on marriage, he would tell her when he was ready and not before.

The Manor rose up against the dawn sky—it looked almost threatening. It made Jared's whole body tense beside Clara in the back of the car. Only she knew how he must be feeling at this moment. Her hand closed over his and she looked up at him, worried for him.

But he returned her gaze steadily. He wasn't afraid.

Or, if he was, he'd rather die than show it. And meanwhile the car was crunching gravel on the drive as it pulled up slowly in front of the fading steps.

'Are you coming in?' Gareth appeared to be blissfully unaware of the emotional time-bomb he was inviting with those casual words. 'I'll get some coffee for us all.'

'Thanks,' Jared said in a rough voice, and a second later was out of the car, standing in front of the Manor.

He stared up at it with justifiable trepidation. But as Clara stood beside him she saw the determined thrust of his jaw and recognised that steely look—she had seen it a thousand times before, every time he had a big deal going on, was about to take a crazy gamble and knew by instinct alone that he would win.

'Come on!' Gareth halted at the top of the steps to look back at them in surprise. 'This way.'

'On second thoughts,' Jared said with restrained emotion, his voice slurred as he stared at the open double doors, 'hold the coffee. I'd like to be alone in the hallway with Clara for a few minutes. Would you mind?'

Gareth frowned, perplexed. 'Sure, okay…' Gareth gave a wry shrug. 'Why not? Just come along to the dining room when you're ready.' He went away, dismissing his curiosity as he started whistling.

When the hall was empty, and all they could hear was the rush of the sea and the cry of gulls, Jared said, 'I didn't look when we were here before. I couldn't look. I looked away. I looked at the sea. I looked everywhere but through those damned doors…'

His whole life had been leading to this moment, since the violence and tragedy had erupted, destroying his childhood, setting him on the road to fame and fortune—then bringing him full circle back to the place where it all began.

'I don't know how best to go in,' he muttered thickly, then looked down at Clara, and before she could reply suddenly swept her off her feet.

'Oh…!' Her arms went around his neck as he carried her up the steps and over the threshold like a bride.

'Can't think of any other way but to carry you in!' he drawled, and then they were in the great hall.

They stood in the centre. Cavernous dusty walls rose all around them. The breeze whispered in through the open doors, just as it had for decades, and the chandelier tinkled softly in greeting, as though it had been waiting for Jared Blackheath to return.

'Just a hall. Just a house,' Jared said under his breath, and his voice echoed softly as he stared up at the ceiling.

His black evening suit was afire with the blaze of her long red gown as he stood rigidly, holding her like a bride in his arms. Clara remained silent, watching his face as she kept her arms around his neck, waiting until he felt safe enough to put her down.

'This is where I stood when I first came in,' Jared said deeply. 'It all looked so much bigger then. Twenty times the size of this. I felt dwarfed by it.

More helpless than I can ever remember. Overpowered completely by this house, this hall...'

'You were a little boy,' she said gently. 'And you were in a state of extreme shock.'

'I feel as though I'm still in shock. Nothing seems real. And at the same time—it's all horribly real.'

Slowly, he set her down on her feet. Then he walked towards the stairs, started to climb them one by one, each step measured. Retracing the past, every inch of it, he was determined to confront the ghosts of childhood full in the face.

Clara picked up the skirt of her long red gown and ran to join him. They climbed the rest of the stairs together. The minstrels' gallery loomed long and dusty before them. Footsteps echoed on the stone floor below. Jared stopped, and they both looked down to see Owain Llewellyn walking into the hall from the dining room.

Owain had not seen them. He did not turn his silver head to look up at the minstrels' gallery until he reached the centre of the hall. Jared and Clara presented a strong, united front to the old man. They shone with beauty, glamour and power. Gone were the young lovers, both vulnerable, and in their place stood a tycoon and a famous actress.

'Forgive me for intruding,' Owain said. 'I've been up since the hospital called with the good news.'

'Susie's on the road to recovery,' Jared said. 'We were with her when she woke up. It's nothing short of a miracle.'

'Yes, and I stayed up because I was so excited. I was just waiting for Gareth to come home, that's all.

But when he came back, when he told me you were here…*here*, Jared, here in the hall…'

Jared studied him with guarded eyes and said nothing.

'I'm sorry,' Owain said. 'But I had to see it for myself. I never thought I'd see it. I only wish your mother could—' He broke off.

There was a long pause.

'You wish my mother was here to see it?' Jared's strong dark voice echoed in the old hall, and with it three decades of silence was finally broken for ever.

'I'm sorry,' Owain said again, 'I didn't mean to say that. It just came out. So stupid of me. I'm such an old fool, I—'

'No,' Jared interrupted him. 'It was time I came back. I'm glad I did. And you're right. My mother should be here to see it.'

With a double-take, Owain blurted out, 'I—I could telephone her now! She's awake, just as we all are, so pleased about Susie. I only spoke to her a few minutes a—'

'Well, go on, then,' said Jared. 'Give her a call. Tell her to get in her car and drive on over.'

'You don't mind if I bring her back to this house? After all that happened here because of us? Because of what we—'

'See her with my blessing.' Jared pushed away from the balustrade and walked back along the gallery, holding Clara in the crook of his arm. 'See her as often as you want. I won't stand in your way.'

'Oh, my boy!' Stumbling towards him, Owain

stretched out his bony old hands. 'My very dear boy! We felt so guilty for so many years—'

'No need to explain.' Jared waved him away as he reached the bottom of the stairs. He was prepared to forgive and forget. He was happy to see them reunited in this house. But he didn't want any emotional scenes. Not yet, not just yet…

'No. Of course…' Owain nodded, bowed his head and stepped back.

Jared looked at him for a long moment, then said deeply, 'Just take it as written that I've forgiven and forgotten.'

Owain looked up at him with a grateful smile.

Jared smiled too, and the sun came flooding into Rhossana Bay, across the grounds of the Manor and into the hallway itself.

'Besides,' Jared said, 'your wife died last year and my mother's still a widow. You're both here again, back in the same area. What could be more natural than for the two of you to get back together again?'

Owain's eyes had filled with tears, and as Jared walked past him towards the open double doors he called, 'I'll tell her to come right away! I need her to hear all this from you!'

'She can't today, I'm afraid.' Jared turned in the sunlit doorway with a regretful smile. 'Clara and I have to fly to London right away.' He turned to smile down at her as she stood safe in the circle of his arms. 'Isn't that right, darling?'

'The test!' she gasped. 'Oh, Jared! We completely forgot to ring Mitch and tell him I couldn't—'

'Serendipity,' he drawled, kissing her. 'Now we

can fly to London together, you can test for
Rachel—and we'll be back here in Wales in time
for dinner!'

CHAPTER TEN

THE helicopter flew them straight to London. They'd had time to rush back to the hotel, grab a bite to eat, make love in the shower *and* get dressed. They were both fairly wired—they had neither of them slept. But Clara was alert with adrenalin despite the lack of sleep and the series of emotional shocks she'd sustained in the last twenty-four hours.

'At least they were all positive shocks,' Jared commented as they flew over London. 'And the adrenalin will help you get through the test.'

'I feel so alive. Are my eyes red?'

'Faintly. Just explain what happened last night. They'll understand that your red eyes are only temporary.'

The chopper circled the helipad of the Blackheath International skyscraper. It was one of the tallest buildings in the City.

'You'll sail through the test,' Jared reassured her.

'I don't know about that! I can barely remember any of my lines. I feel as though I've been through a whirlwind. It's wiped my memory banks clean!'

'You *have* been through a whirlwind,' he drawled, smiling. 'But you're a professional, you've done this a million times before, and you'll remember your lines the minute the cameras roll.'

'I hope you're right.'

'Of course I'm right,' he said with an arrogant smile. 'And meanwhile I'll wait right here for you at the office. It's a perfect opportunity to march in, shake 'em all up and get things rolling again.'

The helicopter landed with a gentle thud on the top of his skyscraper. He got out, gorgeous in a grey business suit, fresh white shirt, jade silk tie and gold cufflinks. Turning, he helped Clara out too, and she kissed his clean-shaven jaw as he held her in his arms, dark hair blowing as the blades from the chopper whirred and the wind blew across the city skyscrapers.

'Yummy!' she murmured against the fresh scent of aftershave and clean skin. 'I wish we could go home to bed!'

'We will do,' he said thickly, kissing her and holding her close to the warmth of his body. 'Just as soon as we get back to Wales.'

'Mr Blackheath!' Men in suits came running.

'A crisis has blown up in the Sydney office!'

'I'll be with you in a minute!' Jared called coolly, then turned back to Clara, grimacing and lowering his voice. 'They can't seem to run this place without me. What are they going to do when I go back to Wales tonight?'

'Pine for you,' laughed Clara, arms wrapped around his strong neck. 'Just as I do, every time you go away.'

'Well, that won't be for some considerable time. I don't want to let you out of my sight again if I can possibly avoid it...' His mouth closed over hers in a brief, burning kiss.

A moment later they were walking hand in hand

across the roof towards the grey doors which led to the main building. Jared waved the men in suits away, motioning them to keep their distance as he went into the top floor with Clara.

'Take a cab straight back here once the test is over.'

'Are you sure?' She kept pace with him as they entered the Chairman's suite of offices—his, naturally. 'I can easily just go back to Regent's Park.'

'What's the point of that? The chopper's here.'

'Mr Blackheath!' His personal assistant came running up—a woman in her mid-forties with black hair and a stern face. 'Thank heavens you're back!'

'Briefly.' Jared paused in the luxurious champagne-coloured corridor. 'And I'll be with you in a minute, Mrs Radcliffe. I just want to see Miss Maye to the lift.'

'Wonderful to see you again, Miss Maye,' Mrs Radcliffe enthused. 'Am I to understand congratulations are in order?'

Clara and Jared exchanged shocked glances.

'Congratulations?' demanded Jared curtly. 'What are you talking about?'

Mrs Radcliffe went white. 'Nothing sir. Nothing. I—I have made a mistake. Do forgive me...' She blundered away to her office.

Jared led Clara to the Chairman's lift, muttering, 'She must have been talking about Susie getting better.'

But as she looked up into his strong face she saw the telltale stain of dark red on his cheekbones and was suddenly sure he was lying. But why? And about what?

'Come on, you'll be late.' Jared hurried her into the expensive mirrored lift and waved as he stood outside it, smiling. 'Good luck! Break a leg! See you back here later—'

The lift doors closed, cutting short his last words. Clara stood trembling against the mirrors. Her adrenalin levels were so high that she could barely think properly. Too little food, low blood sugar, not enough sleep, a recall test to face—and now all this business about congratulations being in order. Congratulations about what? Perhaps Mrs Radcliffe *had* been talking about Susie, she told herself. Yet that didn't explain Jared's anger or the dark flush on his face. But there wasn't time to think.

As soon as she reached the ground floor, security men were waiting with walkie-talkies and dark glasses to lead her across the palatial foyer of Blackheath International to the limousine waiting for her outside in the busy City street.

Whisked to the television centre, she was rushed through Hair and Make-up, hassled through Wardrobe and finally emerged on set at one-fifteen, looking stunning in a blue evening gown, to play a multiple character scene at a tense and emotional dinner party. She felt as though she'd been trampled over by a herd of elephants. But her adrenalin began to pump as soon as she heard those magic words:

'Speed…'

'Turning over…'

'And—action!'

Her head lifted, her stomach clenched with excitement and the lines came back to her.

Suddenly she was Rachel, interacting beautifully with the other actors at the dinner table. Her voice throbbed with emotion. Her eyes blazed with genuine feeling.

'Perfect.' The director smiled admiringly at her when the scene ended. 'Off you go. I'll just have a quick word with Mitch...'

Clara went back to Wardrobe alone, leaving Mitch talking to the director in the corner of the sound stage. After changing back into her smart ivory skirt-suit, she unpinned her chignon, ran her fingers through her long blonde hair and sighed.

Why was everything so up in the air at the moment? Jared's feelings about marriage were very much unsettled, for all her hopes in Rhossana. Susie was out of danger but still not recovered from her injuries. And the role of Rachel, for all that she'd rushed here by helicopter and limousine, was still not hers.

'Can I get those falsies back, Miss Maye?'

Clara looked up in surprise as the make-up lady popped her head round the door. 'Oh, yes...!' She peeled the false eyelashes off with a wry smile. 'I thought I looked weird!'

'And the grips?'

Scooping up the hairgrips, Clara handed them back. The make-up lady disappeared. Seconds later, there was another knock on the door. Don't tell me, she thought, laughing, she wants all the make-up back too.

'Are you decent?' Mitch shouted, and she sighed with relief.

'Oh, it's you! Yes—come on in.'

He burst in through the door like the dynamo he was, all perfectly coiffed hair, expensive Italian suit and razzle-dazzle smile. 'You were brilliant! You were Rachel! You've got the part!'

'What?' Clara stared at him in acute shock. She couldn't quite believe it could be so easy to hear those words. She'd heard them a hundred times before— 'You've got the part'—but with Rachel somehow they seemed more life-changing than they ever had before.

'Yep. The director just told me. I'll have official confirmation in the post tomorrow, but other than that—you *will* be Rachel.'

'Oh, I must get back to Jared and tell him! He'll be so thrilled!'

'No need, darling. I spoke to him a couple of minutes ago on my mobile. He already knows.'

'You spoke to Jared?' Clara stared at him in amazement. 'You mean—you rang him?'

'No, he rang me.' Mitch smiled and kissed her cheek. 'We had quite a long chat. He explained why it was so difficult to phone through to you in Wales. He's so proud of you, Clara. You've got a good man there. Hang on to him.'

Mystified, Clara had to bite her lip to stop herself asking Mitch for more information. Jared would never forgive her if she gave so much as one more piece of his private jigsaw puzzle to Mitch, and, given how tired and off balance she was, it was far too dangerous to spend any more time standing around here talking to Mitch.

The limousine took her straight back to Blackheath

International. As she entered the building the security men were waiting to escort her to the Chairman's lift. Jared always made sure his staff treated Clara like a visiting princess, but today they appeared to be going overboard.

What's going on? she wondered as she rode up alone. First the peculiar congratulations from Mrs Radcliffe, then the strange call to Mitch, and now the security men falling over themselves to pamper her.

The lift doors slid open. The luxurious offices were deserted. Puzzled, Clara walked to the outer offices but found nobody there. He must be in a meeting, she thought, and has probably taken Mrs Radcliffe with him.

Going into Jared's private office, she found that, too, deserted.

Where was he? The big black winged leather chair stood empty behind the vast leather desk covered in telephones. Behind it, there was a panoramic view across London; from here Jared was able to look down on the whole City—the little boy from Rhossana Bay had made it very big indeed.

A smile touched her heart. What an amazing man, she thought. To have made it so high, to have come so very far, and with such tragedy to surmount. Clara had always been proud of Jared's towering success, but now she'd seen his home town it seemed even more incredible that he'd done so well. If only his father were here to see it, she thought sadly. But, if his father had been here, would Jared have become the man he was?

Clara walked over to the desk and sank down in

the black winged chair. Twirling around, she imagined herself as Jared, looking out of this window,
master of all he surveyed. No wonder the people in
Rhossana stared and whispered when they saw him.
No wonder they—

Her gaze fell on the ink-blotter on the desk.

'Mrs Clara Blackheath,' Jared had written in bold
black pen. 'Mrs Jared Blackheath. Mrs J. Blackheath.
Mr and Mrs Jared Blackheath. Clara Blackheath.
Jared Blackheath and Son. Blackheath and Son
International. Clara Suzanne Blackheath and her hus-
band, Jared...'

The sun slanted across the ink-blotter, dazzling the
eye with the whiteness of the paper and the stark black
handwriting across it. Such strong writing. Such
self-assurance. What had he been thinking as he wrote
all that? Her heart skipped a beat, for she knew there
was only one answer, just one...

To her right, the door clicked open.

Clara looked up, stunned and silent.

'Hi.' Jared stood in the doorway, devastatingly
handsome in his grey suit, sunlight gleaming off gold
cufflinks and jet-black hair. 'I hear you got the part.
How do you feel?'

Wide-eyed, she just stared at him.

'Cat got your tongue?' he drawled softly, and came
in, closing the door behind him with a click.

'No, I was just...' She stared down at the ink-
blotter again. 'I was just...'

'Just reading something on my desk?' His voice
was cool and arrogant, but as he strolled lazily towards her his fists were clenched and she could sense

his heart thudding much too fast. 'What did you read?'

'My name...'

He stopped beside her, looking down through heavy-lidded eyes. 'My chair, I believe.'

Clumsily, she got to her feet.

'Thanks,' he drawled lightly, slid into the powerful chair and tugged at her wrist with one hand, making her fall onto his lap.

'Oh...!' Breathless, she landed on him, hands against his broad chest, staring up into his tough face and feeling absurdly nervous for some unaccountable reason.

'I was doodling,' he said thickly, holding her with hands that seemed to tremble fractionally, 'while I was on the phone to Mitch.'

'Yes, he said you called him.'

'Just checking that the test was over. Wanted to see how you'd done and when you'd be back here.'

'Ah...' She didn't know what else to say.

'I kept him talking for as long as possible. Asked him a lot of leading questions without giving the game away. I needed to see if you'd told him anything. I should have known you wouldn't have said a thing.' His long fingers played with her blonde hair. 'You look lovely, by the way. I don't think I've ever seen you look so lovely.'

Clara stared into his blue eyes.

'I...' His voice began to shake. He cleared his throat, flushed dark red, looked away. 'I have a present for you.' He reached into his inside jacket pocket.

His hands were shaking visibly now, and his heart was going crazy. 'Just a little something…'

Clara was very still as she saw the small black box in his hands.

'I hope you like emeralds,' he whispered unsteadily, and opened it.

Sunlight blazed over the vast square-cut emerald ring. Surrounded by tiny diamonds, it dazzled the eye, reflecting shards of coloured light all over Clara's pale, excited face.

'It's…it's beautiful.'

'I had someone from Cartier meet me here at one o'clock,' he told her in a thickened voice. 'Didn't want anyone to see me buying a ring for my girl. They showed me every emerald ring they had in stock. In here, behind closed doors. Very discreet! Unlike Mrs Radcliffe, of course, who rather let the cat out of the bag.'

Silently, she looked up once more into his eyes.

His flush deepened. He looked away, looked at the ring. 'Here…let me put it on for you.'

Pulses racing frantically, she let him lift her left hand and slide the ring onto her engagement finger.

Jared whispered, 'Will you marry me?'

'Oh, darling!' she said hoarsely, and fell into his arms, kissing his strong neck, then his determined jaw, moving up as the tears began to sting her eyes until her mouth met his and their kiss blazed with more emotional passion that she had ever felt before.

His mouth was hard and yet tender at the same time as he opened her lips beneath his, crushing her in his arms until she could feel his pounding heartbeat in every inch of her skin.

Breathing hard, he broke off the kiss. 'Thank God for that!' He clasped her head with shaking hands. 'I didn't know how to do it! Didn't know what to say, how to begin…'

'Oh, Jared, I love you so much!' she whispered inanely.

'I rehearsed it a million times but I couldn't get it right. I was so scared you'd say no.'

'How could you think that?'

'Because I'm a man,' he laughed huskily against her pale hair. 'And I hate being vulnerable.'

'I love you this much *because* you're vulnerable. You so rarely show it, yet it's a part of you that makes me weak with love, darling, so weak I—'

'You can afford to be weak. You're a woman.' He touched her face with a strong, loving hand. 'It's so different for me. And, no matter how many times you've made it clear that you like the idea of marriage, I still felt nervous.'

Her smile was tender. 'Is that why you let me see your experiments with our names?'

'I arranged it all very carefully,' he confessed. 'I made sure the offices were deserted. I left you in here for just long enough. I knew you'd sit in my chair. You always do when I'm not around.'

Tears stung her eyes. 'It's such a wonderful chair…'

'Just as I knew you'd read our names. I figured if you read them and didn't want to marry me, I'd know as soon as I walked in.'

'I've wanted to marry you since the day we met!'

'People can change their minds, darling. I was so afraid that you might have changed yours.'

'But I was never the one against marriage.' She lifted her head to stare in wonder at him. 'It was always you. I can't believe you've even asked me. When did you decide? What happened to change your mind?'

'You happened,' he said deeply. 'You. I started to change the minute I met you. I knew it even as it was happening. But it was such a slow, gradual process, Clara. Everything started to unravel the night we met, but there was so much to unravel that it's basically taken the full two years to get me to this point. And you were right. It *was* fate that Susie had the accident.'

'I kept telling you it was fate,' she said with a loving smile. 'I just knew it, even as I was praying for her to recover and railing against the terrible injuries she'd suffered. But everything seemed to fall into place from the minute you arrived in Rhossana.'

'No. It started falling into place before that. Long before Susie's accident. Long before the wedding. It really all began the night I met you and saw myself reflected in your beautiful eyes.'

'Ah…' She studied him.

He smiled, reading her expression accurately. 'Yes. Do you know why I fell so heavily for you in just one night? It was when you told me that your parents had died in a fire when you were eight years old.'

Clara stared into his blue eyes, realising the full impact her words must have had on him. She remembered saying it to him, that was the odd thing. She remembered every second of the night they had met.

'What else did you say, Clara?' he asked, touching her face.

'That my parents had died and that a part of me had died with them for ever,' she whispered, and shivered in his arms as she realised anew the enormity of the love between them, which had sprung up so powerfully that very first night.

'It was as though I'd lived it myself,' Jared told her deeply. Tears sheened his blue eyes. 'I loved you that very first night. And I wanted to tell you my story even then, Clara. It was the first time I had ever wanted to tell anyone. But something in me couldn't. I just…' He looked away, too moved to continue, and she saw the tightening of his mouth as he fought to control his feelings.

'You were too used to living behind that wall of silence.' She said it for him, her voice husky with love.

'Yes, but I knew you were the one. I knew it before we even left the party. I couldn't sleep when I got home. All I could do was remember my own past. I was burning inside with the need to tell you, and thought I'd never be able to do it.'

'I was deeply affected too,' she confessed, holding his hand and stroking the long fingers. 'I remember sitting there, with you, hearing myself say all that and thinking: Why am I telling him all this? What's making me talk this way?'

'You probably sensed a soulmate in me as soon as we met.'

'Oh, yes. I sensed that.'

'And although I couldn't bring myself to tell you about my father, I knew if I could tell anyone, it was you. That's why I insisted you move in with me so quickly. I figured if I kept you around on a daily basis, I'd one day be able to tell you everything. And I hoped, somewhere right at the back of my mind, that telling you would break the spell. That I'd be able to break out of that terrible silence. That I'd be free for the first time. And that some day I'd be able to start considering marriage as a real-life maybe instead of a total impossibility.'

'I can't believe you felt like that from the very beginning.' She was amazed at what had been going on in his complicated mind the whole time she'd been living with him. 'You always seemed so completely against marriage. You said you'd never marry. *Never.*'

'I was used to saying and thinking it,' he admitted. 'But, darling, I'm very human. I wanted love. I wanted you to be mine for ever. I—I wanted children, too.'

'Blackheath and Son International!'

'I need someone to inherit all this.'

'Darling, I'll give you a whole rugby team!'

'I want them born in Wales.' He suddenly pulled her into his arms again, crushing her against his powerful chest, and she listened to his heartbeat as though it were the most important sound in the world.

'Do you want to live there?' she asked his chest.

'I want a home there.' He drew back to look at her, face tight with controlled emotion. 'I want to buy a plot of land on the outskirts of Rhossana. Design and build my own house. And I want it to be the most unusual, beautiful and unique house that's ever been built on Welsh soil! Will you be happy to live in Rhossana? It won't be all year. We'll just go there for weekends, brief holidays—that kind of thing. I can hardly move my whole business empire to a tiny little seaside town in the middle of nowhere. There'd be nothing left for my sons to inherit!'

'I'll be very happy to live there.'

He studied her in silence for a second, then said deeply, 'I want to call our first son Bryn.'

'I think that's a lovely idea.'

'And I'll call the house Blackheath Manor.' He frowned thoughtfully. He'd obviously been planning all this for some time, perhaps since they'd first arrived in Rhossana a week ago. That complex brain had been ticking over all these problems and working out ways around any barriers it found.

'Blackheath Manor sounds lovely,' Clara said, interested to hear more and encouraging him to tell her all his secret plans. 'I'm sure your father would have been very proud if he'd seen it.'

'It's going to be the most unusual design, Clara!' His eyes shone with excitement as he felt and responded to her encouragement. 'I've already figured it all out!'

Clara smiled, knowing full well that he had.

'A towering white house with a central square surrounded by spherical towers, and turrets and triangular wings extending on four sides.'

Her eyes widened. 'Goodness! What on earth will the townsfolk think of it?'

'That it belongs to Jared Blackheath,' he drawled, with an arrogant glint in his eyes. 'Built and designed by him, worth millions and sitting in the middle of fifty acres of the richest land in all Rhossana!'

'What a wonderful monster you are!'

'And,' he enthused, 'I'm going to commission a twenty-foot-tall oil painting of my father from the best artist in Europe! Bryn Blackheath when he was young, well-loved and the most handsome man in town. I'll have it hung at the top of the grand staircase once the house is built.'

'And then throw a big party,' she suggested, 'inviting all Rhossana as well as half the most famous, glamorous and wealthy people in the land?'

'Stop pinching my ideas!' he drawled, and kissed her nose.

Clara laughed softly and then said, 'Is that how you want our wedding to be, darling? Full of the glitterati and—?'

'No.' He grew serious again. 'But, on the other hand, I don't want it to be conventional. I couldn't handle it, Clara.'

'The paparazzi?'

He shuddered, then looked uncertainly at her and said in a halting voice, 'I—well, I started to think in Wales…'

'Yes, darling?'

'I'd quite like to get married on the cliffs of Rhossana Bay.' He watched her carefully for any sign of disagreement. 'With you in a long white lace dress, barefoot, with flowers in your hair. Very bohemian.

Completely untraditional. And I'd just wear—say, grey trousers and a white shirt. But no jacket, no tie.'

'And who,' she asked with a loving smile, 'would marry us that way?'

'Well, I was thinking of Dai Williams's father.'

'Isn't he the local priest? Would he be allowed to conduct a ceremony like that?'

'So long as it was all above board and totally legal, I don't see that there would be a problem.' He gave a fond smile. 'The seagulls would be our congregation. Gareth and Susie would be our only witnesses. And we would marry at dawn, secretly, so that nobody else knew we were there.'

Clara kissed him. Romantic man, she thought. I knew he was, as soon as I saw those passionate blue eyes. Imagine Jared wanting to get married at dawn on the cliffs overlooking a Welsh sea. Most people would see him marrying at a sophisticated city cathedral, with hundreds of guests going on to an expensive party at an even more sophisticated hotel.

'Would you be happy with that?' he asked deeply.

'Delighted,' she said, kissing him.

'Of course, we'll have to fit it around your filming schedule.' He frowned, that complex brain starting to tick over the problems again. 'You'll be filming this series for five months, won't you? And then I'd want to make you pregnant…'

Her heart somersaulted with love. 'Yes…' Her fingers linked with his. 'Pregnant right away. As soon as the cameras stop turning I want to start making babies with you.'

'What if you win the award, though?' He studied

her anxiously. 'It might make you discontent to just be—'

'I've always wanted to be barefoot and pregnant for you, darling. Ever since I met you. What makes you think an award for Best Actress will change that?' She slid her arms around his neck, pulled his head down towards her to kiss him, and murmured against his lips, 'I'm a woman before I'm an actress. I'd much rather win Best Lover, Wife and Mother Award from you than anything anyone else could ever give me...'

His mouth burned down passionately over hers, and as she returned his kiss wholeheartedly she thought how wonderful life could be if you just followed your feelings, remained patient, trusted fate and believed in true love.

She'd always wanted children. Just the thought of being pregnant was suddenly more wonderful than any other thought she'd had. Next thing on the list, she thought with delirious happiness, is to be barefoot and pregnant...

And eight months later, she achieved her goal.

She also won the coveted gold statuette for Best Actress, but Baby Bryn rather disgraced himself when he was two by trying to feed it to the dog.

DANCE FEVER

How would you like to win a year's supply of Mills & Boon® books? Well you can and they're FREE! Simply complete the competition below and send it to us by 31st October 1998. The first five correct entries picked after the closing date will each win a year's subscription to the Mills & Boon series of their choice. What could be easier?

OBLARMOL
AMBUR
RTOXTFO
RASQUE
GANCO

KOPLA
OOOOMTLCIN
MALOENCF
SITWT
LASSA

EVJI
TAZLW
ACHACH
SCDIO
MAABS

G	R	I	H	C	H	A	R	J	T	O	N
O	P	A	R	L	H	U	B	P	I	B	W
M	O	O	R	L	L	A	B	M	C	V	H
B	L	D	I	O	O	K	C	L	U	P	E
R	K	U	B	N	C	R	Q	H	V	R	Z
S	A	N	I	O	O	N	G	W	A	S	V
T	S	I	N	R	M	G	E	U	B	G	H
W	L	G	H	S	O	R	Q	M	M	B	L
I	A	P	N	O	T	S	L	R	A	H	C
S	S	L	U	K	I	A	S	F	S	L	S
T	O	R	T	X	O	F	O	X	T	R	F
G	U	I	P	Z	N	D	I	S	C	O	Q

D8C

Please turn over for details of how to enter ⇨

HOW TO ENTER

There is a list of fifteen mixed up words overleaf, all of which when unscrambled spell popular dances. When you have unscrambled each word, you will find them hidden in the grid. They may appear forwards, backwards or diagonally. As you find each one, draw a line through it. Find all fifteen and fill in the coupon below then pop this page into an envelope and post it today. Don't forget you could win a year's supply of Mills & Boon® books—you don't even need to pay for a stamp!

Mills & Boon Dance Fever Competition
FREEPOST CN81, Croydon, Surrey, CR9 3WZ
EIRE readers send competition to PO Box 4546, Dublin 24.

Please tick the series you would like to receive if you are one of the lucky winners

Presents™ ❏ Enchanted™ ❏ Medical Romance™ ❏
Historical Romance™ ❏ Temptation® ❏

Are you a Reader Service™ subscriber?   Yes ❏   No ❏

Ms/Mrs/Miss/Mr ....Intials ....
(BLOCK CAPITALS PLEASE)

Surname...

Address ....

....

....Postcode........................

(I am over 18 years of age)   D8C

Closing date for entries is 31st October 1998.
One application per household. Competition open to residents of the UK and Ireland only. You may be mailed with offers from other reputable companies as a result of this application. If you would prefer not to receive such offers, please tick this box.   ❏

Mills & Boon is a registered trademark of
Harlequin Mills & Boon Ltd.